Patience for Love

Editing by Joanne LaRe Thompson

Patience for Love

By
Jennifer Skinnell

A Hope Springs Romance

About the Author

Hello, I'm Jennifer Skinnell. I'm a quilter, travel blogger, the mother of two wonderful adult children, grandma to two adorable boys, and wife to a wonderfully supportive husband. I loved creating the town of Hope Springs with all its quirky characters of the Advice Quilting Bee. My pages may not be steamy, but I hope they make you laugh and fall in love with the residents of Hope Springs.

Be sure to check out One Sweet Development, the first installment in the Hope Springs Romance Series, also available on Amazon.com.

When I'm not writing, I'm quilting. For access to my world, check out my website www.jenniferskinnell.com

Follow me on:
Facebook: Jennifer Skinnell, Author
Instagram: @jenniferskinnellauthor @theramblingquilter
Blog: www.theramblingquilter.com

Acknowledgments & Dedication

Thank you to my family and friends for your continued support while I tell the story of the ladies of the Advice Quilting Bee. I'm forever grateful to each and every one of you for your encouragement and assurance that what I'm writing is worth reading. As I continue to delve deeper into the ladies' lives, bits and pieces of my own past come to life on the page. So if something seems familiar to you, please know that it was with love that I included it in my story.

And to my editor, Joanne LaRe Thompson, thanks so much for your continued guidance!

I dedicate this to every Rosie and Myrtle in the world who just want to help the younger generation find love and happiness.

To many, quilting is just putting two pieces of fabric together with a layer of batting between and making something to keep warm on cold winter nights. In colonial times, quilting Bees were gatherings of women around large quilting frames, hand stitching the fabric pieces together while socializing and supporting one another.

Today, many quilters have turned to machines in their sewing rooms to produce quilts faster but losing the social aspect of quilting in the process. The ladies of Hope Springs have embraced the art of hand quilting, and as a result, socializing, supporting, and advising each other is a large part of their weekly gatherings. They have come to be known as the Advice Quilting Bee.

The Ladies of the Advice Quilting Bee

Rosie Macintire – Matriarch and Founder of the Advice Quilting Bee, owner of Rosie's Quilting Emporium, widowed, two children: Robert, the Hope Springs Bank President, and Ramona, deceased

Mary Ann Macintire – Married Rosie's son, Robert; works at Rosie's Quilting Emporium

Missy Macintire – Mary Ann's daughter, works at Everything's New Again Boutique

Chandler Bradford – Engaged, owner of Sweet Stuff Bakery

Myrtle Freeman – Rosie's best friend and fellow quilter, unofficial president of the Little Old Lady Network, six grown children, including Ben, the Hope Springs Fire Chief

Candy Freeman – Married to Myrtle's son, Ben; works part-time at Rosie's

Luann Freeman – Candy's daughter, a college senior who works at the bakery in the summer

Fran Mayfield – Owner of Hope Springs Mercantile & Ice Cream Shop, member of the Little Old Lady Network, divorced, no children

Macy Greenburg – Chandler's best friend and neighbor, nurse at the Hope Springs Medical Center

Hillary Smith – Owner of Everything's New Again Boutique, married to Jack, two children

Andrea Porter – Owner of Hope Springs Diner, widowed, no children

The Town of Hope Springs

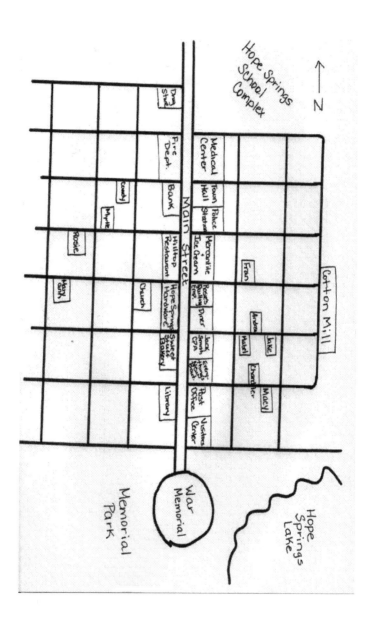

Prologue

"Honestly, Macy, what do you think of this one?" Chandler Bradford asked her friend, Macy Greenburg, as they shopped for a wedding dress. Chandler was engaged to Peter Frederick, and the wedding was set for the first weekend in November, only a short ten weeks away. "I need to find something off the rack."

"I think it's lovely," Macy said absently.

Chandler turned from the mirror. "Macy, are you even looking at this dress? You seem to be a million miles away."

Macy came back to earth. "I'm sorry, Chandler." She took the time to look at the long lace gown that, in reality, looked like it belonged on her grandmother's dining room table. "Um, do they have something with a little less lace?" she asked, waving her hand over the dress.

Chandler smirked. "A little too much like something Rosie would have on her dining room table?"

"I was going to say my grandmother, but Rosie is good too," Macy laughed. "As your maid of honor, I feel it's my duty to make sure you aren't wearing a tablecloth on your wedding day. Let's see if there are any other options," she suggested. As Chandler went back to the dressing room with the bridal consultant, Macy went in search of something more modern for her best friend.

Macy pulled an elegant strapless A-line number with a sweetheart neckline and bling around the waistline. She took her selection to Chandler and ordered her to try it on even though she wasn't looking for strapless. "I know you

9

aren't looking for this style, but try it anyway," Macy insisted, handing the dress to Chandler.

As Macy waited for her friend to emerge from the dressing room, she reflected on how her life had changed in a very short two years. She had landed what she thought was her dream job working for a dreamy doctor in the city. The hours were great, with no nights and no weekends. But about six months after she started, the dream fell apart, and she'd been forced to quit.

Macy soon learned of the Hope Springs Medical Center opening and jumped at the chance to begin a new life in the sleepy little town of Hope Springs. She rented an adorable cottage that happened to be across the street from Chandler, and they hit it off immediately. The best thing was, the doctor she was working for was an older married guy—kind of like working for her grandfather.

Things were going great in her small-town life until Dr. Howard decided to retire and hired Dr. Jake Grainger to take his place. He was nothing like her grandfather, and given her past history, she wanted to stay as far away from him as possible. Not an easy feat in the office, but she thought she could do it after hours. That was until Chandler informed her that since he was her fiancé Peter's best friend, he would also be the best man. Ugh!

Chandler stepped out of the dressing room in Macy's pick. She was positively glowing, and the dress fit her like a glove. "Macy, maybe you missed your calling and should have been a bridal consultant. It's perfect!" Chandler exclaimed through a mist of tears. She turned to face the mirror.

"You are stunning," Macy whispered through her own mist of tears. "It doesn't even need any alterations."

"So, based on your reaction, can I assume this will be your wedding dress?" asked the consultant, smiling.

Chandler stared at herself in the mirror and almost didn't recognize the woman staring back. "Yes," was her answer.

"Perfect!" the consultant shouted, clapping her hands. "Now," she said, turning to Macy, "How about a dress for the maid of honor?"

Macy looked at Chandler. "We hadn't discussed what I would be wearing. Do you have any ideas of style or color?" she asked.

Chandler thought for a minute. "Well, we're getting married in the new gazebo Peter is building in the park. How about something tea-length? As for the color, I'm thinking about a rustic wedding theme with merlot, peach, and sage green. With your red hair, peach would probably not work. Let's see something in either the merlot or sage," she decided, turning to the consultant.

"Give me a few minutes to pull some dresses. I'm guessing these will also have to be off the rack since it usually takes close to twelve weeks to get ordered dresses in," the consultant explained.

Macy and Chandler agreed that would be cutting it too close. While Chandler went into her dressing room to change from her wedding dress, Macy chose another room to get ready to try on her choices. Soon, the consultant handed her two of each color in different styles. Macy decided to try on the sage dress with spaghetti straps and a sweetheart neckline, similar to Chandler's gown. As she was zipping up the back and looking at herself in the mirror, she couldn't help but notice her first thought was about what Dr. Grainger would think of her in this dress. *Bad idea, Macy!*

She exited the dressing room to show the first choice to Chandler. As Macy stood on the podium looking at her reflection in the three-way mirror, she decided this color didn't do much for her red hair.

Chandler's face was saying pretty much the same thing. "Not your color. You need something that is going to make you irresistibly gorgeous, not blend in with the fall foliage."

Macy smiled. "Yes, but the point is not to upstage the bride. I'm supposed to blend in with the scenery."

"Oh, no," Chandler shook her head. "I'm not one of those brides who need to have all the attention focused solely on them. If you're going to give so much of your time to be in my wedding, I'm going to make sure people remember you were there as well. Try on one of the merlots."

Macy was so happy Chandler wasn't one of those bridezillas. She had several friends in college who had been like that, and she hated being in their weddings. They expected only the best of everything and wanted their bridesmaids to pay a fortune. She returned to the dressing room and removed the sage dress.

Next up was a strapless merlot tea-length dress with an organza overlay. It also had a sweetheart neckline and was cinched at the waist by a rhinestone belt. Macy thought it did amazing things to her figure. She liked this one and hoped Chandler approved. Once again, she had that fleeting thought of Dr. Grainger but quickly pushed it out of her mind.

"Oh, this is the one," exclaimed Chandler when Macy walked out of the dressing room. "You are stunning in this one. And it's very similar to mine."

"You're okay with it looking so much like yours?" the consultant asked. Most of her brides *wanted* their bridesmaids to blend in with the scenery.

"Oh, yes," Chandler answered, looking at Macy, who was beaming in the mirror. "I want my best friend to feel as beautiful as I do on my wedding day."

"Wow, you two really do have a special friendship," remarked the consultant. "I'm guessing you have known each other all your lives."

Macy and Chandler started laughing. "Believe it or not," Macy answered, "we've only known each other a little over a year. But I've never been closer to anyone than this wonderful person here."

The tears were back in Chandler's eyes. "The feeling is mutual. I was so happy when Macy moved in across the street from me. She and I have gone through many bottles of merlot on my front porch over the past year."

"Well, then I think the merlot dress is perfect," said the consultant with a hint of a tear as well.

Macy hugged Chandler and said she couldn't agree more. Both were also happy that they had completed this vital task so quickly. A little less than three months wasn't a lot of time to get a wedding together.

Chapter 1

If anyone had told Jake Grainger a year earlier, he would be moving to a small town and running a medical center, he'd have thought they needed to see a psychiatrist. And yet, here he was. He had moved to Hope Springs a few weeks before to take over the practice from the retiring doctor who just happened to have grown up in this small town. And while Dr. Howard had known every one of his patients, Jake knew none of them. But he was up for the change and the challenge.

Since the move had been somewhat sudden, Jake hadn't had time to find a place to live, not that there were many options in Hope Springs. His best friend, Peter Frederick, had introduced Jake to his grandmother, Rosie Macintire, who he soon found out, was the community's matriarch. She owned and operated Rosie's Quilting Emporium, as well as owning a lovely four-bedroom Victorian home that had been in her family for generations. Rosie was more than happy to have Jake stay with her until he could find other accommodations.

As luck would have it, Peter was moving back to Hope Springs to marry the local baker, Chandler Bradford. And as a real estate developer, he planned on turning the old Cotton Mill into condominiums, so Jake was looking into the possibility of purchasing one.

"Good morning, Jake," Rosie greeted him as he came downstairs. "I have fresh blueberry muffins and fruit if you're interested."

"Rosie, that sounds heavenly," Jake said, hugging her. "But as I've tried to tell you, you don't need to cook for me. I'm very grateful to you for opening your home to me, and I don't want to be an inconvenience." Peter had mentioned to Jake that Rosie had just turned eighty-four years old. He didn't want to be a burden.

"Not in the least," Rosie said. "It's nice having someone to cook for. Now, if you're looking for a gourmet meal, you've come to the wrong place. But if a good, home-cooked meal is on your mind, then I'm your girl. Would you mind helping me with this tray and carrying it out to the veranda? It's a beautiful day, and I thought we could have our breakfast out there."

"I'd love to," Jake said, looking at his watch, "And since I don't have to be at the medical center for half an hour, we have time." Jake was still getting used to the idea of opening at nine o'clock in the morning, and also the fact that it only took him five minutes to walk to work.

As they got situated on the veranda, Jake took a look around. Rosie's home faced north, so the veranda was in the shade most of the day. Since it was August, the sun could be brutal, even at this early hour. Another thing Jake noticed was how quiet it was. He grew up in the city and learned to tune out the noise. However, sitting there he could hear a lawn mower starting up, birds chirping back and forth, and somewhere in the distance was the sound of children playing. He could get used to this.

"So, Jake," Rosie interrupted his thoughts, "What do you think of our sleepy little town?" She took a bite of the muffin she had just buttered.

Jake took a moment to take a sip of coffee. "I was just thinking about how quiet it is. There are so many sounds I hear that I'd probably tuned out when I lived in the city."

Rosie shook her head up and down. "Yes, the times I've been to the city to visit Peter, I do remember it being quite noisy. I enjoy just sitting here and listening to life."

Jake thought about that. "Yes, that's what it is. Life." Peter had told Jake his grandmother had such an interesting soul, and he was looking forward to getting to know her. He took a bite of the homemade blueberry muffin and washed it down with another sip of coffee.

"You know, Jake," Rosie began, "Hope Springs is a very special place. People come here thinking they will only be staying a short time. Then they end up spending the rest of their life here. The town reaches in here," she said, placing her hand on her chest, "and wraps around your heart. We're also a very close community, and we look out for one another."

Jake looked at Rosie. "Why are you telling me this?" Had he done something already to offend a resident or one of his patients?

"Oh, you haven't done anything wrong, if that's what you think I mean," explained Rosie. "You know about the Advice Quilting Bee, right?" she asked.

"Yes, Peter told me about it," he said. A group of women got together at Rosie's shop every Thursday night to work on hand quilting a quilt for a very deserving cause from what Peter had told him. Over the years, the group was been known to dispense advice about life and relationships to anyone who needed it, whether they were quilting or just visiting. Thus the name—the Advice Quilting Bee.

16

"Well," Rosie continued, smoothing out her floral print dress over her knees, "your name has been mentioned recently. Of course, one reason is that you are the new young good-looking doctor in town."

Jake smiled shyly at that. He wasn't sure he was okay with the description, but oh well.

"And the other reason is that some of the older ladies in the group think you would be a good match for our Macy Greenburg," she finished. She picked up her coffee and looked at him over her cup for his reaction.

Jake didn't know what to say. Macy was one of his nurses. She was also the one who wouldn't give him the time of day. "Rosie, there must be some mistake. Miss Greenburg will barely speak two words to me in the office unless it relates to a patient."

Rosie smiled. "First of all, you might start by calling her by her first name. We're a small town, after all. And secondly, I understand your concern. Our Macy came to us just over a year ago from the city. I can't put my finger on it, but there was a reason she came here. I don't pry into others' personal lives, and she hasn't opened up, but I believe her spirit has been wounded." Rosie placed her hand over Jake's. "My advice to you is to be patient. Your wanting to have a relationship with Macy, professional or otherwise, will warrant patience."

Jake looked at Rosie's eighty-four-year-old hand on his and thought about how many others she had counseled over the years. In the short time he'd known her he could tell she was a woman of great integrity and wisdom, as well as someone with a very generous heart.

Jake placed his other hand on top of Rosie's. "Thank you for the advice. Right now, I'd just like for her to talk to me without looking like I'm going to attack her," he smiled.

"Patience," Rosie cautioned. "Patience."

Jake thought about his conversation with Rosie as he walked to work. He wondered what could have possibly happened to Macy to make her so shy around men. Or was it just him? That he wasn't sure about. He'd have to start paying more attention.

As he reached the front door of the medical center, Jake noticed the waiting room was packed. A quick look at his watch told him it was just nine o'clock, so he wasn't really late. As he hurried inside, he saw the frantic look on the face of his receptionist, Suzie. Jake raced back to his office to grab his lab coat to begin what looked to be a hectic Monday morning.

Chapter 2

Macy woke up Monday morning to the incessant sound of her alarm beeping. She would have thrown it across the room if it hadn't already been there. She'd learned long ago that if she put her alarm on the nightstand beside her bed, it was too easy to keep hitting the snooze button. If it was across the room, she had to get up to turn it off, and therefore, was less likely to go back to bed.

After turning off the alarm, Macy walked down the hall to the kitchen and turned on her coffee pot. She was still one of those who brewed a pot in the morning. She had to watch every penny, and it was far cheaper to use the old-fashioned kind than it was to use one of the newer one-cup varieties. She did, however, find a four-cup version. Of course, since she used a travel mug, it was more like a two-cup version.

Macy continued with her morning routine of taking a shower, dressing in her scrubs for the day, and getting caught up on the news. While sipping her "home" cup of coffee, she poured the rest into her travel mug. She looked in her cabinet to see if anything appealed to her for breakfast. Of course nothing did so she decided to stop by the bakery to pick up something yummy. Already feeling guilty for the calorie intake, she made a salad to take for lunch.

Taking a quick look around to make sure everything was tidy and that the coffee pot was turned off, and Macy was ready for the day. Since it was early August, she was hoping for a slow day at the medical center. In another week, they would be busy with kids getting check-ups and shots before heading back to school. With her luck, though, there would have been a flu outbreak in Hope Springs over the weekend, and they would be lined up at the door.

Macy locked the door to her rental cottage and stepped out into a very warm August morning. *Darn, should have gone with iced coffee today,* she mused. She looked across the street to see if there were any indications that Chandler was still home. Determining that she had probably gotten to the bakery early, Macy walked the two blocks to Main Street and the bakery. She loved this time of the morning. It was quiet and peaceful. She also loved this small town, and now that she'd been here over a year couldn't think of living anywhere else.

Macy could smell the cinnamon rolls before she had even entered the bakery. Since she was arriving before their nine o'clock opening time, she tapped on the front door. She could see Chandler's assistant, Luann Freeman, look up and smile.

"Good morning, Macy," Luann said as she unlocked the door and stepped back for Macy to enter. "How are you this morning?" she asked, locking the door once more.

"I'm good, Luann," Macy replied, "but very hungry. I figured I'd be just in time for a warm cinnamon roll."

"Anything for my maid of honor," Chandler shouted from behind the counter. She came out with a hot cinnamon roll handed it to Macy along with a fork. "Let's have a seat at the table so you can enjoy."

"I think I have time," Macy said, looking longingly at the cinnamon roll. "I'm not the only nurse today. And Mary will be so busy flirting with Dr. Grainger that she won't even know I'm gone."

"Isn't Mary about sixty and married?" asked Luann.

"Yep," Macy answered, in between bites. "Doesn't matter. She still thinks he's going to come to his senses and do whatever with her."

"And how does that make you feel?" asked Chandler, watching her friend intently.

Macy put her fork down and looked at Chandler. "Well, Dr. Bradford, I really don't care what they do. I'm just there to do my job and collect my paycheck. I don't feel the need to flirt with the doctor to do that. I'm totally fine with keeping our relationship strictly professional."

By now, Gretchen, Chandler's other assistant, had come around to the front of the display cases. "You know, Macy, if I didn't know better, I'd say you are a wee bit jealous of their relationship."

Macy's mouth dropped open. "I am not!" she denied incredulously. "I don't want anything more than a professional relationship with Dr. Grainger."

Chandler placed her hand on Macy's arm. "You know, not all doctors are like the ones in the city. And I happen to know this one pretty well already. He might be worth your time of day."

Macy looked at her watch. "Oh, darn, would you look at the time." As she got up, she turned to Luann. "Put the cinnamon roll on my tab. Gretchen, it was delicious as usual."

When she tried to turn toward the door, Chandler stopped her. "You know what I'm talking about," Chandler whispered, so only Macy could hear. "History doesn't always repeat itself."

Macy looked at her best friend. "But sometimes it does." She hugged Chandler and walked out the door Luann had just unlocked to open for business.

As Macy crossed Main Street and continued walking toward the Hope Springs Medical Center, she passed Rosie's Quilting Emporium. She'd been going there every Thursday evening for the Advice Quilting Bee, partly for the wonderful dinner provided, partly to learn the art of hand quilting, but mostly for the feeling of belonging she got when she was with the ladies. However, since Dr. Grainger had moved in, he seemed to be the main topic every week.

Besides quilting, some of the older ladies had taken it upon themselves to become the town matchmakers. She had seen it in action with Chandler and Peter, and unfortunately, it seemed she was their next target. There was only one person in the group who knew about her past, and that was Chandler. She knew Chandler would keep her secret but she was worried the rest would start trying to pry it out of her. With Chandler's wedding coming up, she was going to try to steer the conversation in that direction at their next meeting.

Macy entered the Hope Springs Medical Center a few minutes later to find a waiting room full of patients. Suzie, the receptionist, had a harried look on her face, and Mary was running around like crazy. As Macy looked around, the common thread among the patients was that they were all senior citizens. "What's going on?" Macy asked Suzie.

"It seems there was a bad batch of something at the senior center dinner last night," Suzie hurriedly responded.

"Food poisoning?" Macy asked incredulously while she looked around the waiting room.

"Not sure," Mary shouted from the back. "Not all of the patients are showing signs of that. Dr. Grainger is just beginning to examine them."

Macy quickly took her things to the back room and came out to help Mary get the patients sorted out. Her job was to ascertain swiftly what they ate to see if there was a common thread. Since Macy knew some of the women, she really wanted to know just what was going on.

She headed straight to the one who was usually the spokesperson of the group. "Myrtle, can you tell me just what happened last night that could get all these people sick?"

Myrtle Freeman straightened her bright floral top over her double-knit slacks. "Well," she started, "as far as I can tell, we all ate different things. Isn't that right, Fran?" she finished, looking over at her friend, who was also the owner of the Hope Springs Mercantile.

"Yes," Fran Mayfield agreed, chewing on the stem of her reading glasses dangling from her neck on a beaded chain. "It was also a buffet, so it could be tough to figure out."

Macy looked at the group. Then she got up and walked over to Mary. "Just what are their symptoms anyway?"

"Well, they were all kind of vague," Mary explained. And then, noticing the strange expression on Macy's face, she asked in a hushed voice, "You don't think they're faking, do you?"

Macy looked around the waiting room. The common thread with all the women in the group was that they were all part of what Chandler loved to refer to as the Little Old Lady Network. And they were up to something. But what could it be?

When Dr. Grainger came out of the examining room with Mabel Clark, she had her answer. "Honestly, Mabel, I can't find anything wrong with you," he was explaining as he handed her chart to Suzie.

"Oh, but Dr. Grainger, are you sure? I'm feeling a little flushed," Mabel said dreamily and actually had the nerve to put her hand to her forehead for good measure.

Macy watched as all the other ladies started fanning themselves as if they had the same flushing symptom Mabel was experiencing. It was all Macy could do not to roll her eyes. Then she had an idea.

"You know, Dr. Grainger," she began, loudly enough for everyone to hear, "I remember we had a patient with similar symptoms when Dr. Howard was here. I can't quite remember the diagnosis, but Dr. Howard thought the holistic approach was best to treat the illness."

"Really?" asked Jake, trying not to smile. "And just what was the holistic treatment?"

"I believe the treatment for this particular illness was a teaspoon of castor oil," Macy said, looking at the group.

Seeing their shocked expressions, Jake announced, "Well, if that's what Dr. Howard recommended, then that's what I'll prescribe." He turned to Mary. "Please write a script for each of these lovely ladies. I think that one teaspoon ought to do the trick, but put to repeat every hour as needed until they feel better."

Mary tried hard not to smile. "Yes, Dr. Grainger," she answered, beginning to write the first prescription.

Mabel was the first to crack, as Macy had known she would. "Oh, no, I'm not taking castor oil. Myrtle, this was another one of your harebrained schemes, so you can have mine. I'm out of here!" And with that, Mabel practically ran from the medical center, along with all the other ladies, except Fran and Myrtle.

Myrtle walked up to Macy. "That was not a very nice thing to do to a group of old ladies," she said, wagging her finger at her. "Come on, Fran, let's go," she bellowed as she headed toward the exit.

"Right behind you, Myrtle," Fran told her fellow conspirator. But before she walked out the door, she looked back at Macy. "Well played child, well played," Fran said as she placed her leopard print sunglasses on the bridge of her nose. Smoothing her ruffled top over her long floral skirt, she gave them all a big grin before she exited.

Macy, Mary, and Suzie started laughing, and Jake decided there was some joke that he wasn't in on. "Okay, ladies, what was that all about?" he asked.

"You have just had your first encounter with the Little Old Lady Network of Hope Springs," answered Mary. "You're now officially welcomed into our community."

"That," Jake asked, pointing to the door, "is this town's version of the Welcome Wagon?"

"More like our non-internet version of social media," Suzie explained.

"Yes," agreed Macy. "If you need anything to be told all over town in a matter of minutes, just let one of them know. And beware of their spies. They have them all over town as well, including some of their husbands. There are no secrets in Hope Springs."

Jake looked at Macy for a minute. "Oh, I'm sure there are a few secrets those women don't know about."

Macy just smiled shyly. She wasn't sure how to answer that one. Fortunately, the door opened, and in walked their first actual appointment of the day.

"Saved by the bell, so to speak," whispered Jake, so only Macy could hear.

Why did that simple action send shivers down her spine? *Not good*, thought Macy, *not good at all.*

Chapter 3

The rest of the day was relatively calm. Aside from little Billy Green breaking his arm falling out of a tree, it was pretty quiet. At closing time, Macy was cleaning up Exam Room One when Jake walked in. He took a moment to look at her dressed in light blue scrubs with puppies printed on them and wondered what she would look like in a pair of jeans and a t-shirt. He was sure that somewhere under all that baggy clothing was a great figure. He shook his head to clear that thought as she turned to face him.

"Oh, hi!" Macy said, startled. "I'm almost done in here if you need the room." She checked the last drawer to see if she needed to refill any supplies.

Jake put his hand up as if to stop her. "No, you're fine," he answered. "I was just going to ask if you knew whether the diner was still open. Rosie had said she was going to be going to her son's for dinner—not that I expect an eighty-four-year-old to cook for me every night." He wasn't sure why he just kept talking, but for some reason, he was nervous.

"Let's see, today is Monday so that means it's homemade meatloaf and mashed potatoes at the diner," Macy told him. "Andrea is open every evening until eight, except Sunday when she closes at six o'clock." There were two restaurants in Hope Springs. The Hilltop was more formal and somewhat stuffy. The Hope Springs Diner, the more casual of the two, was owned and operated by Andrea Porter, who was also a member of the Advice Quilting Bee. Macy personally liked the diner more.

"That sounds delicious," Jake gushed, his mouth watering at the thought. "I hate to eat alone. Would you care to join me for dinner?" He knew he was going out on a limb, but for heaven's sake, it was just dinner. Jake could see the hesitation and slight look of panic on Macy's face. "Maybe we could see if Peter and Chandler would like to join us and discuss plans for the wedding."

Macy tried not to let out the breath she didn't realize she'd been holding. "I'll text Chandler to see if they're free," she said with a smile while pulling her phone from her scrubs pocket.

"I have a few more things to finish in my office," Jake replied. "Let me know when you hear from her," he said before heading back to his office.

Macy sent a text to Chandler and then went back to finishing up the exam room duties. She felt her phone vibrate and looked down. Chandler said they were free and would meet them at the diner in half an hour. She also added that Macy should relax because it was "just dinner". Macy smiled at that because she was just thinking the same thing. Chandler really did know her too well. Macy sent her a thumbs-up emoji.

"Come on, Macy!" Mary shouted from the front door. "Let's go!"

Jake popped his head in and asked, "Are we all set for dinner?"

"Yes," Macy answered, looking around the room to make sure she'd done everything. "Chandler and Peter are going to meet us there."

"Great. Let's close up and go before someone else shows up," he said, waving his hand for Macy to lead the way down the hall.

The four of them left the building, and Jake locked the door behind them. As Mary and Suzie headed toward the parking lot behind the building, Macy thought she heard Mary say something about her and Jake going on a date, but she chose to ignore it.

"Construction on Peter's new office building is coming along," Jake observed, making conversation as they walked. "I know he wanted to be done as soon as possible so he could move his company headquarters here."

"Yes, that's what Chandler said. I'm so glad he's moving here instead of her moving to the city," Macy replied. As they were walking, Macy noticed a familiar group of women sitting in front of the bank across the street. *Oh great*, she thought, *they probably think we're on a date.*

Jake had noticed the same group. "Don't look now, but the Little Old Lady Network is watching us," he said, chuckling. He was beginning to love this sleepy little town.

"I noticed that, too," Macy acknowledged, a bit irritated. "I'm sure I'll be hearing all about how I walked up the sidewalk with Dr. Grainger, so of course, we must be getting married."

Jake couldn't believe they would carry it that far. "Married?!" he asked incredulously.

"Oh, yes," answered Macy, quite serious. "Those ladies live vicariously through the younger generation of Hope Springs. Beware of little old ladies carrying handbags on their arms."

Jake started laughing. Not just chuckling but laughing.

Macy stopped walking. "What's so funny?" she asked, clearly having missed a joke somewhere.

Jake stopped as well and turned to look at her. "Beware of little old ladies carrying handbags on their arms— *really*?!" he asked, trying to stop laughing.

"That's fine. You can laugh," Macy said as she started walking again. "But don't say I didn't warn you." As they reached the diner and Jake held the door open for her, she looked back across the street and saw Myrtle with a big smile on her face. *Not good,* she thought, *not good at all.*

They entered the diner and found that Chandler and Peter had beaten them there. Peter got up to hug Macy and shake Jake's hand. "I'm so glad you all thought to come here tonight," Peter commented. "Chandler was threatening leftovers," he said with a wink.

"Hey," Chandler said, gently hitting him on the arm. "Before you came along, I would have been perfectly content with a bowl of cereal, followed by a glass, or three, of wine with Macy on the front porch."

"That's right," Macy agreed, smiling. "And sometimes we just skipped the cereal and went straight to the wine."

Jake already saw a different, more relaxed side of Macy. And it made him even more curious about just who the real Macy was. "Well, I, for one, am way too hungry tonight to have a bowl of cereal." The waitress, Alicia, came to take their drink orders and let them know the specials, but Jake stopped her by putting his hand up. "I already know that if it's Monday, it's meatloaf and mashed potatoes. I'll have that and a glass of sweet tea."

"Yes, sir, Dr. Grainger," Alicia smiled. "I'm guessing you all want the special," she stated, looking around the table. They all nodded in agreement. "Sweet tea, as well?" Again, they nodded in agreement. "Thanks so much. I'll be back with your drinks."

"So, I hear your morning was quite interesting," Chandler started the conversation.

"How did you hear about our morning?" asked Jake.

Peter chuckled. "Jake, you'll learn real quick how news travels around this town. And it doesn't involve the internet."

"Ohhhh," Jake said, understanding. "Well, I'm sure by now everyone in town knows we're here having dinner, and they probably think Macy and I are on a date."

Chandler got a sympathetic look on her face. "Uh, oh. I take it the Little Old Lady Network saw you walk in here together."

"Yes," Macy answered. "Myrtle was smiling from ear to ear. Honestly, we really need to find something else for them to do."

"I thought they spent all their time making quilts?" Jake asked.

"That's only on Thursday nights," Macy explained, "and then we're there with them. Fran runs the mercantile, but I think she must have summer help because she's never there.

31

Mabel volunteers at the visitor's center, but it closes at four, and Myrtle helps out at Rosie's Quilting Emporium, but only on Saturday. The rest of the time, they're spying on all of us."

"And as we found out, they also have spies all over town," Peter interjected. "Get used to it, my friend."

Jake smiled. "Actually, I like living here. I've never been more relaxed."

As Alicia delivered their drink order, Jake asked, "How are plans coming for the condominium complex? I'm so grateful to Rosie for letting me live with her, but I don't want to be a burden."

"First of all," Peter began, "Rosie would never think of you as a burden. Second, we just finished the site inspection, and the architect is developing the plans now. But it's still months away from completion."

Seeing the look of disappointment on Jake's face, Chandler said, "You know, one of the homes on the street behind me is almost finished being remodeled, and I know they are looking to rent it out. Maybe you should look into it."

Macy had a momentary thought of panic but then realized that Jake would be living a street over from her. "That's a nice two-bedroom model like ours, isn't it, Chandler?" she asked.

Jake liked the sound of that. "With two bedrooms, I could make one my office. Thanks, Chandler. I'll look into it tomorrow." He wanted to get into his own place soon.

Their dinners arrived, smelling heavenly. "I have died and gone to Heaven," Jake stated after taking a bite of meatloaf. "This is amazing."

"The Hilltop may be fancier," Peter commented, "but the food here is so much better."

"If I keep eating like this every night, I'm going to outgrow my clothes quickly," Jake said, tapping his stomach. "Is there any kind of gym or exercise place here?"

Chandler chuckled. "Just Myrtle's exercise class at the church on Friday mornings."

Jake looked at her with a puzzled expression. "Why is that so funny?"

"I don't think that class is really for Jake," answered Macy, chuckling as well.

"Okay, what's wrong with it?" Jake asked, clearly wanting to know the joke.

"Oh, nothing is wrong with it," Peter told him. "It's fine if you're over sixty-five."

"Explain, please," Jake pleaded, looking at Chandler.

"Well," Chandler began, "Myrtle and her friends get together and exercise to one of those eighties videos. And they actually have a VHS tape player. No DVD for them!"

Jake stared at her. "You're kidding, right?"

"Nope," answered Macy. "And if you're lucky enough to see Myrtle before or after class, you'll see her spandex outfit, complete with matching shoes and headband. It's a sight for sore eyes," she finished, trying not to laugh.

Jake just continued to stare. "And trust me," Chandler continued the explanation, "she isn't kidding me when she says 'sore eyes'."

"A little bright?" Jake asked.

"Lime green florescent isn't as bright as what Myrtle has been seen in," Chandler answered. "She showed up at my house early one morning, and I almost got a headache just looking at her."

"Okay, then. Clearly, that class is out of the question," Jake said. "Are there any other options for exercise around here?"

"Well," Peter began, "you could always go to the high school and see if you can use their weight room. And they have a nice track for running."

"Hmm, I guess I may have to do that since there aren't many other options." Jake decided. "Maybe once you move here permanently, Peter, we'll have to look at a way to change the exercise mentality of the town. Since I am the town doctor, I feel it is my civic duty to provide a healthy place for people to exercise."

"I like the sound of that," Peter agreed. "Of course, I am marrying the fabulous town baker, so we might have an uphill battle on our hands," he said, laughing.

"Well, if you two come up with a place for us to exercise and keep fit, Macy and I are all in!" Chandler announced.

Macy stared at her. "Wait a minute! Why am I getting roped into this?"

Chandler tapped her on the arm. "Because you are the town nurse, my dear. You should be setting a good example."

By now, everyone had finished eating, and Alicia was asking if anyone cared for dessert. "I would like a piece of chocolate cream pie," Macy announced. Seeing the rest of the table look at her with shocked expressions, she defiantly said, "If you people are going to make me start getting healthy, I'm going to enjoy my pie while I still can."

"I'm with Macy," Chandler agreed, "Chocolate cream pie for me, too."

Peter and Jake looked at each other and followed suit. The women just shook their heads.

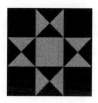

Chapter 4

"Here, Fran, go try this on," Hillary Smith said, handing Fran a flowery, peasant dress with ruffles around the top and bottom. Hillary owned the Everything's New Again Boutique. She always made sure that if something came in on consignment that she thought one of the women of the quilting bee would like, she held it for them. "I also have a couple of skirts that just came in you might like. I'll go to the back and get them."

"Thanks." Fran was eager to try on her latest finds. Fran was a self-professed child of the sixties and loved the flowing tops and skirts of the era. She was so happy when they came back in style recently. "Let me start with this while you look for the rest," she told Hillary, heading into the dressing room.

As Fran was emerging from the dressing room, Hillary was coming from the back with the skirts. "I found a couple of tops that might go with them," she said, going past Fran to hang them in her dressing room.

"I think I like this one," Fran told Hillary, turning to see herself in the three-way mirror.

"That looks great on you," Hillary approved. "It's the right length and everything."

"Let me see how the rest look, but I definitely want the dress. It's fancy enough to wear to Chandler and Peter's wedding," Fran decided, lightly brushing the ruffle detail around the neckline with her hand. "I could even maybe attach a little lace up here to dress it up even more."

"That would be really pretty," Hillary agreed.

Fran went back into the dressing room to try on the next outfit. Once all was said and done, she ended up with everything, the dress, two tops, and two skirts. "These are great, Hillary!" Fran exclaimed. "And I know I couldn't have found them for a better price anywhere else."

As Hillary finished ringing up the sale and carefully folding the garments to put in a bag, she thanked Fran for coming into the shop. "My goal is to make my customers happy and at a fair price."

"We ladies have to stick together to make sure our businesses thrive," Fran agreed. "It's an exciting time around here, what with all the new business Peter is planning on bringing to the town, and everything."

"I know. Business is definitely looking up," Hillary acknowledged. "So, I hear you spotted our resident doctor going into the diner with our favorite nurse last night."

Fran sighed, "Myrtle made too much of a very innocent evening. According to Andrea, they met Chandler and Peter there, and that was all there was to it. He didn't even walk her home."

"I figured it was something like that," Hillary said, smiling. "For whatever reason, Macy doesn't want to have much to do with Jake. Not sure why, though. He's so nice and not bad to look at either."

Fran picked up her bag from the counter. "I feel bad for the girl. You know how Myrtle can be when she sets her mind to something. And she has her mind set on the two of them getting married."

"Married?!" exclaimed Hillary. "Isn't it a little too soon for that?"

"Not with Myrtle, it's not," Fran told her, shaking her head from side to side. "I think it's going to be up to the rest of us the protect Macy until she's ready to reveal whatever it is she needs to reveal."

"Yeah, I think you're right," Hillary agreed. "Thursday night's quilting bee ought to be interesting."

"Always is," Fran said as she headed out into the intense afternoon heat. She got back to her shop just as Myrtle was going in. "Hey, Myrtle, want to cool off with some ice cream?" she asked.

"Hi, Fran," Myrtle answered. "That sounds delicious. It certainly is hot today," she said, brushing her curly red hair off her face. "Find anything good at Hillary's?"

"As a matter of fact, I found two tops and skirts to match. Plus a dress I can wear for Chandler and Peter's wedding," Fran answered, stashing her bag behind the counter. "What flavor will it be?" she asked, opening the ice cream case and picking up a scoop.

"Hmmm, let's go with strawberry today," Myrtle decided. "I'm not sure what I'm wearing to their wedding, but we still have over two months to decide. I guess it'll depend on the weather since everything will be outside."

"Cup or cone?" Fran asked.

"Cone," Myrtle replied. "But, you know, theirs may not be the only wedding we'll be needing dresses for."

Fran stopped scooping and looked at Myrtle. "Oh, is there something you're not telling me?" she asked, kind of sheepishly.

"Not me!" exclaimed Myrtle. "Macy and Jake!"

Fran just shook her head and continued scooping. She handed the cone over to Myrtle and began scooping a strawberry cone for herself. "Now, Myrtle, don't start in on poor Macy like you did with Chandler," Fran chastised. She finished her own cone, and they headed over to the table set up in front of the window. As they sat down to eat their ice cream, Fran added, "The girl can barely talk to Jake, so I don't think we should have them walking down the aisle just yet."

"Now, Fran," Myrtle started, between licks of strawberry ice cream, "was I not right about Chandler and Peter?" She picked up a napkin from the holder to wipe excess ice cream from her lips.

"Yes, you were," agreed Fran. "But this is different. Chandler at least talked to Peter, even if she didn't like him at first. Macy will barely look at Jake. I think the poor girl has something she's not disclosing about her past, and that's why she's so skittish around him." Almost as soon as the words were out of Fran's mouth, she knew she shouldn't have said them. She could see the wheels turning in Myrtle's head and knew she would be determined to find out about Macy's past.

Fran held up her free hand. "Myrtle, you leave Macy alone. Just because she has a secret doesn't mean you have to find out what it is."

But it was too late. Myrtle's wheels were turning faster than ever. "Well, maybe the Advice Quilting Bee can help poor Macy get over her past," Myrtle declared. "Of course, we'll have to know just what it is we need to help her get over. I wonder if she has confided in Chandler?" she asked, turning her cone for another lick before it melted all over her hand. "Maybe I'll pay a visit to Chandler before Thursday night," she stated.

Fran shook her head from side to side. "I wish you would just let this go," she advised. But Fran knew Myrtle was like an old dog with a bone. There was no use trying to talk sense into her because she was set in her ways. "Okay, if I can't get you to let this drop, at least try to be discreet about it. Macy probably doesn't want everyone to know her story. Otherwise, she would have told all of us by now."

"Now, Fran," Myrtle said, finishing the last bite of her cone, "I'm nothing if not discreet."

"Uh-huh," answered Fran, sarcastically.

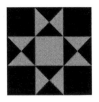

Chapter 5

"*Bang, bang, bang!*" Chandler sat straight up in bed and looked over at her clock.

"*Bang, bang, bang!*"

"What in the world?!" Chandler said aloud as she rubbed her eyes. "Who is banging on my door this hour!?" She got out of bed and peered out the bedroom door toward the front door. Her shoulders slumped. "Myrtle." She reached for her robe on the hook behind the door and tromped to the front door. After unlocking it, Chandler threw it open and all but shouted, "Myrtle, what do you think you're doing, banging on my door at six o'clock in the morning!?"

Myrtle actually dared to look upset with her for shouting. "Chandler, you shouldn't shout at an old woman. I could have a heart attack or something," she said, rubbing her chest.

"Myrtle, you and I both know you are one of the fittest residents of Hope Springs. Why are you waking me up this early?" Chandler noted that Myrtle's outfit of choice was a hot pink, sparkly, floral top with matching hot pink capris. She was also wearing flashy, hot pink flip-flops.

"Aren't you even going to invite me in?" Myrtle asked, clearly thinking that six o'clock in the morning wasn't too early for a social call.

Chandler stepped aside for her to enter. "Would you like me to make your coffee and breakfast as well?" Chandler asked somewhat sarcastically.

Myrtle shook her finger at Chandler. "You know, I would have thought you'd be a more gracious hostess, Chandler. Honestly, it's not that early."

Chandler decided it best just to play along. Clearly, Myrtle had something on her mind, and knowing her, she had been up all night thinking about it. "Okay, what's so important that you couldn't wait until I was at least up and dressed?"

"Well," Myrtle began, "You know our new doctor, Dr. Grainger?"

"Yes," Chandler answered, "we've met." Chandler noticed that Myrtle seemed a bit nervous and decided to have a little fun with the woman who woke her up so early. "Why?" she asked. "Do you have a crush on him?" she asked, stifling a yawn.

"Honestly, Chandler, I don't think this is the time to joke," Myrtle replied. "Poor Macy needs our help."

Chandler made her way to her kitchen situated in the back of her two-bedroom cottage. She figured she was going to need coffee to deal with whatever crisis Myrtle had made up. After turning on the coffee pot, she turned to Myrtle. "Just what does Macy needs our help with?"

"Getting over her past, of course!" Myrtle practically shouted.

Chandler turned back to the coffee machine and began preparing herself a cup. She knew for a fact that she was the only one who knew the details of Macy's past and was stalling to see if Myrtle was bluffing. Once her cup was full, she turned back to Myrtle. "So what do you propose we do to help Macy?" she asked as she took a seat at the kitchen table. If Myrtle knew about Macy's past, this would be the time she'd find out.

"That's why I came to you, Chandler," Myrtle stated, sitting opposite Chandler at the table. "Do you have any ideas on how we can help her?"

"Well," Chandler began, taking a sip of her coffee, "Why don't you ask Macy? Has she said she's interested in Jake?"

"Well, no," Myrtle sighed. "But I've seen the way they look at each other, and I know there's chemistry there."

"Really?" Chandler asked curiously. "Peter and I had dinner with them the other night, and I didn't pick up on that at all."

"Oh, that's because you were too busy looking into Peter's eyes to notice, I'm sure."

Chandler chuckled. "You know, Myrtle, you really are a romantic, but I don't make a habit of gazing into Peter's eyes in public. And especially when we're eating."

"Well, I'm telling you that Macy and Dr. Grainger would make a great couple," Myrtle assured her. "We just need for Macy to come out of her shell. Are you going to help me or not?"

Chandler shook her head from side to side. "Nope. You're on your own with this one. And if Monday morning's trip to the medical center was any indication, your friends in the Little Old Lady Network aren't going to back you up anymore, either."

Myrtle waved her hand at Chandler. "Oh, I don't need them to back me up. If Macy's dear friends won't come to her rescue, then I'll do it on my own," she said adamantly.

Chandler finished the last of her coffee and got up to put her cup in the sink. "Well, you can count me out. And it's time for me to get ready for work. Let me know how it all turns out," she finished as she ushered Myrtle toward the front door.

"Oh, I will," Myrtle replied, walking out into the warm morning sunshine. "I will."

Chandler watched her go down the stairs, smiling. She had no doubt Myrtle would be working on this full-time now. She had to make sure she warned Macy to be on the lookout. But for now, she needed to get ready to head to the bakery.

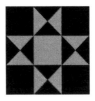

Chapter 6

"As you can see, the cottage has been completely renovated," stated Roger Samuels, the portly real estate agent who was showing Jake the two-bedroom home Chandler had recommended. "There is nothing you would have to worry about as far as repairs or maintenance. Other than mowing the lawn, of course."

Jake looked around the newly updated kitchen. "Yes, I can see it has everything I would need. And you can't beat the price. When would it be available?"

"Immediate occupancy," Roger informed him. "You sign the papers today, I give you the keys, and you can be moving in whenever you're ready. I can make sure the cable, phone, and utilities are all turned on whenever you say so."

"Phone? Of course, there would be landlines here," Jake smiled, answering his own question. "In the city, I didn't have one, but as the town doctor here, it might not be a bad thing to have in case of emergency."

"Yes, I would agree with you," Roger said, pulling a contract out of his briefcase. "So, is this going to be your new home?"

Jake looked around a little more before asking, "Do you know if the owners would be interested in a lease/buy option? I would rather put my money toward potential ownership."

A smile came across Roger's chubby face. "They would prefer that." He reached back into his briefcase and pulled out a different contract. "Here's the lease/buy contract," he said, handing the small stack of papers to Jake. "Feel free to look it over, but it does give you the option of purchasing the home after one year."

Jake took the contract from him and looked it over. He'd rented enough times to check for the usual wording. Satisfied with what he read, he took the pen from Roger's hand and signed the contract.

"Wonderful!" exclaimed Roger, shaking Jake's outstretched hand. "I'll get the ball rolling, and you, young man, can start packing." He looked at his watch. "Since it's past four o'clock, I won't be able to get the utilities taken care of until morning. Would that be okay?"

"That'll be fine," Jake assured him. "Since today is Thursday and the middle of a work week, I won't be able to move my things from my storage unit in the city until Saturday. I'm sure Rosie won't mind having me for a couple more nights."

"If I know Rosie, and I have for almost fifty years," Roger insisted, "she'll be sad to see you go."

"I've enjoyed her hospitality, but I don't want to overstay my welcome," Jake explained.

Roger shook Jake's hand once more and said he'd let him know in the morning once he'd taken care of everything. He handed him the keys and said his goodbyes.

After Roger left, Jake walked into what would be his new office. He was happy the owners had painted everything in a nice cream color. He'd been to Chandler's cottage, and, aside from the fuchsia door, the inside of her home was also done in soft tones. Jake was looking forward to bringing his furniture into the space. He had a brief desire to know what Macy would think of his decorating style. *Why should you care?*

For now, since the air conditioning wasn't on, it was getting too hot to stay inside. Jake went out onto the front porch, which faced north and was more shaded. He could see putting some chairs and a small table out there to have his morning coffee or a beer in the evening. And the nice thing was that he could practically see the medical center. No more long commutes. He liked that.

Jake locked the door behind him and sat on the front step. Taking out his cellphone, he pushed the speed dial for Peter.

"Hey, buddy," answered Peter. "What's up?"

"Wanna help me move on Saturday?" Jake asked, mentally crossing his fingers. He hoped Peter would say yes.

"Absolutely!" Peter exclaimed. "Are you renting the cottage Chandler mentioned?"

"Yep. I'm sitting on the front porch now," Jake said, smiling. "I need to bring everything down from my storage unit in the city. Know where I can rent a truck on such short notice?"

"Don't worry about renting one," Peter replied. "I have plenty of company trucks that'll be available on Saturday. If

47

you supply the pizza and beer, I may even be able to get a couple of my men to help."

"That'd be great," Jake said, smiling. "But since there isn't a pizza place within ten miles, how about dinner at the diner on me."

"That works too," Peter agreed. "Just text me the time and place, and we'll be there."

"Thanks, man," Jake said. "It's nice to have a best friend with trucks and a moving crew."

"Anything for you," Peter commented. "Anything for you."

After they hung up, Jake texted Peter the info. He was feeling really good about his decision to move to Hope Springs, and more importantly, this house. Then his thoughts went to Macy.

Jake had dated more than his fair share of women over the years, and none were this shy around him. No, not shy; skittish was more like it. What could have possibly happened to cause such a reaction every time they were in the same room? He was attracted to her and wanted to get to know her on a more personal level. But he wondered if he would ever be able to crack the protective shell that surrounded her.

During one of his front porch conversations with Rosie, she had advised him to take it slow, and he just had to remember that. He hoped that Macy would slowly begin to relax and feel more comfortable around him if he did.

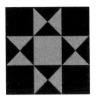

Chapter 7

"Alright, ladies," Rosie began, addressing the ladies of the Advice Quilting Bee. "Tonight, we're continuing our work on the quilt for Katrina Smith. She was supposed to be coming home at the end of August but had a relapse. She'll now be coming home at the end of September, so that gives us more time. We have about six weeks to finish everything, including binding."

Usually, the ladies worked on hand quilting a quilt to be auctioned off for charity. However, this particular quilt was being given to a local resident who was wounded in combat and had been recovering at the VA Hospital. As was customary, Rosie and Myrtle had pieced the quilt top by machine. Mary Ann, Rosie's daughter-in-law, had marked all the stitching lines on the quilt top for the members to follow. Then, at the weekly Thursday night meeting of the Advice Quilting Bee in Rosie's Quilting Emporium, the ladies would have dinner and complete the task of hand quilting the design.

As everyone settled in to work on their section of the quilt, Andrea Porter remarked on what a special gift the quilt would be for Katrina. "That poor child has seen more than her fair share of tragedy. I lived through my husband dying of cancer, but I'm sure it's nothing compared to what she's lived through."

"I know," agreed Hillary, sadly. "The abuse I endured from my ex doesn't seem so bad when you think about what Katrina's seen and lived through."

Rosie looked at the two younger ladies seated across from her. "You have both been through your own brand of hell, but you came out of it relatively unscathed and stronger from it. I think that, as a group, we each have our own strengths we can offer to Katrina when she returns home. Lord knows she's going to need all the love and support she can get."

Macy looked around at the wonderful group of strong women seated at the quilting frame. Each of them had made such a great life for themselves through hard work and determination. Besides Andrea and Hillary, her best friend Chandler had lived through her parents' deaths to a drunk driver when she was little, then the deaths of her grandparents as they were raising her. But she was strong and had built a thriving bakery business. Several of the others were women who raised children who went on to be successful in their own right. Their legacies would live on for generations.

Macy wondered what her legacy would be. Only one of the women in the room knew about part of her past, and that was Chandler. And even she didn't know everything. Macy wasn't sure why she didn't share all the details of her life with her best friend, but something held her back. It wasn't that she was ashamed of all of her past, only parts of it. She just chose to keep most of her life a secret from everyone. She was proud, however, of the fact that she had put herself through nursing school. She had learned early on that if she wanted anything good in life, she had to take care of it herself.

"I'll bet that was a crazy Monday morning, Macy," Macy heard Andrea say as she was finishing that thought.

She looked up from her stitching to see everyone looking at her.

"My goodness child," Fran said, putting her needle down. "You look like you were a million miles away."

"Oh, I'm sorry," Macy apologized. "I was just concentrating on my stitches." She knew that it was essential in hand quilting that all the stitches be uniform. She was still learning the skill.

"Fran was just telling us more about your crazy Monday morning at the medical center," explained Mary Ann. "Did you suggest to Dr. Grainger that he prescribe castor oil?"

Macy smiled proudly. "Yes, I did," she answered, looking straight at Myrtle. "I can't believe Myrtle got all those ladies to lie and say they were sick." Myrtle did at least have a guilty expression on her face. "You should have seen how fast poor Mabel caved when Dr. Grainger prescribed that treatment," she said, laughing. "Then the rest couldn't get out of there fast enough."

Fran couldn't help but laugh as well. "Myrtle had finally met her match on that day!"

"Oh, stop," Myrtle admonished. She tried to go back to her stitching, but Rosie was having none of it.

"Honestly, Myrtle. What were you thinking?" Rosie scolded.

"Well," Myrtle began, "I thought it was high time we checked out our new young, hot doctor to see if he was a potential candidate."

"Candidate for what?" Rosie asked.

Myrtle took off her reading glasses and let them dangle on the chain. "For our Macy, of course," she answered, looking directly at Macy.

Everyone turned to look at Macy. "So, Chandler, how are the wedding plans coming along?" Macy asked, trying to distract everyone.

Chandler was just about to help her out, but Myrtle was having none of it. "Oh, no, you don't! We all think that Dr. Grainger would be perfect for you, don't we, ladies?" she asked, looking around the quilting frame for support. Much to her chagrin, everyone seemed intent on focusing on their own stitching. "Come on, ladies, you know you all agree with me!" Myrtle stated loudly.

Macy decided to take the bull by the horns. "Myrtle, first of all, what makes you think I need a man in my life? And second, why should it be Dr. Grainger?"

"Well, everyone needs a man in their life," Myrtle explained. "You're too young to be spending all your time alone. That's what you do when you get to be our age," she said, including Fran and Rosie in her circle of aloneness.

"I don't mind being alone," Fran said defensively. "But Myrtle is right, dear. You are too young to be deciding to spend the rest of your life alone."

"What makes you all think I want to spend the rest of my life alone?" Macy asked. No one had ever asked her that question, so she wasn't sure where they had drawn that conclusion.

"Well," Myrtle began, "you never show interest in any of the men in town. And before you ask how we know this, remember who we are."

"Yes, the Little Old Lady Network," Macy answered. She also knew that if you didn't see them, that meant one of their spies was doing their bidding. There were no secrets in Hope Springs.

"As much as we hate that name," Myrtle said, staring at Chandler, who had come up with it, "yes, we know many, many things. And one of them is that you never go out with any of the eligible men in our town."

"Of course, the fact that no one has asked me out on a date means nothing," Macy countered.

"Would you go if asked?" Myrtle responded.

"Depends on who was doing the asking," Macy answered, somewhat defiantly.

"What if it were Dr. Grainger?" Myrtle hedged her bet.

"Why him?" Macy wanted to know why Myrtle was so interested in getting her together with Jake.

"He's young and handsome," Myrtle said. "How can you turn down a guy who's tall, with light brown, wavy hair, and hazel eyes to match?"

"Well, he's my boss, for starters."

"That doesn't mean much in a small town," Myrtle answered. "Lots of couples in small towns work together."

"I just don't see that working for me," Macy acknowledged, "but thanks for thinking of me." She decided this conversation was getting a little too close for comfort and looked to Chandler for help.

Picking up one Macy's expression, Chandler decided to step in. "Hillary, Fran said she found some unique items at your shop the other day. I'm going to be looking for something to wear on our honeymoon to Miami. Do you have anything?"

"Yes, I just got in some lovely maxi dresses that would look perfect on you," Hillary told her. "I'll set them aside first thing tomorrow before all the high school girls come in. Many of them know I get my shipment in from some of my best consigners on Thursday, so during the summer, they're waiting at the door on Friday mornings."

"Thanks. I'll stop by once the bakery slows down around lunchtime."

"Why Miami, Chandler?" Fran asked.

"Peter has a friend who has a place in Miami Beach, so we are going there."

"That sounds so romantic," Hillary said, enviously.

Good, Macy thought, *no more talk about Dr. Grainger.*

"So, Chandler, I hear you will be having a new neighbor behind you," said Fran.

"Oh, that's right," Myrtle chimed in. "Dr. Grainger is renting that cottage that has just been flipped. And I hear he's signed a lease/buy contract."

"Myrtle, that only happened at four o'clock this afternoon!" Chandler practically shouted.

Myrtle had a smug smile on her face. "I know. Won't be too far from you either, Macy."

Ugh, thought Macy. "I suppose."

"Okay," Rosie said, feeling she must get control of the meeting, "I think it's time we got back to the real reason we're here. And it's not to play matchmaker." She directed the last comment to Myrtle. "Everyone get back to their stitching."

"Yes, ma'am," Myrtle relented, putting her glasses back on so she could see what she was doing.

"Hey, whatever happened to the quilt of the town we pieced for Peter to use when he proposed the Chandler?" asked Andrea. Peter had asked the ladies to make an art quilt depicting the town with changes he had designed as part of the revitalization project. It included the new buildings now being constructed, as well as a revamped park.

"Oh!" exclaimed Mary Ann. "I'm almost finished quilting it on my machine so we can present it to the mayor at the Labor Day celebration. It's going to be hung in the visitor's center."

"That's so awesome!" Chandler said excitedly. "I still can't believe you all pulled off a marathon piecing session and helped Peter with the proposal without me knowing anything. Such a sweet thing to do," she finished, wiping a tear. "See, I still get choked up thinking about it!"

"It was the sweetest proposal ever," Mary Ann agreed.

"I only hope I can find a prince charming like you did," Luann said dreamily.

"You will," Rosie assured her. "There's someone out there for everyone. Usually when you least expect it."

"Macy has already found her prince," Myrtle remarked, looking straight at her. "She is just refusing to accept it."

Macy chose not to look up from her stitching. She just shrugged her shoulders and kept working.

The rest of the time was spent quilting and catching up on other current events in the town. Candy, Myrtle's daughter-in-law, remarked how nice the park would be now that Peter's company was putting in the gazebo/bandstand. "Won't it be nice having summer concerts and the like?"

"Yes," Hillary agreed. "They're also going to be installing a fun new playground with a pirate ship. My kids can't wait for that."

"I know Peter's team is working hard to have it all completed for the Labor Day celebration," Chandler commented. "He's excited to be a part of our small town finally."

"I'm glad to hear that," Rosie interjected. "His mother was so quick to want to leave when she was young."

"Rosie, he's happy that he can spend so much more time with you," Chandler assured her. "He realizes that family is way more important than business."

"So true," Hillary agreed. "Jack and I make sure we have dinner with our children every night. Even if that means Jack is doing more work after they go to sleep."

"Family is everything," Rosie stated. "Work is just the means to provide, and if you live within your means, then you can have the best of both worlds."

Macy listened to the conversation but didn't contribute. These wonderful women had no idea their words were hurting because they didn't know about her past. What she wouldn't give to have had a family growing up, but that just wasn't in the cards.

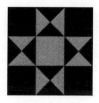

Chapter 8

Saturday turned out to be cool weather-wise, which was a rare occurrence in Virginia in August. Jake met Peter and a couple of his men at his storage unit at seven o'clock that morning. He was glad to see Peter brought a big box truck instead of a pickup. This way, they could get the entire unit unloaded and moved in one trip.

"Thanks for doing this on your day off, guys," Jake said as they started loading the truck. "I'm sure helping me move was the last thing you wanted to do today."

"No problem," the man Peter had introduced as Joshua Burke answered.

"Yeah," the other man, Keith Carson, agreed. "Plus, we were promised good food in return. As two guys who live alone, we don't always get home cooking. Peter claims that's what's in store for us for dinner."

"Like I said, guys, the diner has the best food around," Peter confirmed. "Trust me; you won't be disappointed or go hungry."

As they continued loading the truck, Jake thought Joshua seemed to be about the same age as himself and Peter. Keith appeared a few years older. But they were all in terrific shape. He figured that was because they worked construction.

"So, Keith, how do you like doing construction for Peter?" Jake asked as he packed an end table on top of the sofa.

"Oh, I don't do construction," Keith explained. "I'm his lead architect."

"Yeah," agreed Joshua, laughing. "You'll never see Keith pick up a hammer. A beer maybe, but never a hammer."

"Hey, some of us build, and some of us design," Keith countered. "If it weren't for me, you'd have no reason to pick up a hammer."

"So, I take it you're the construction guy here?" Jake asked Joshua.

"Yep, I'm the contractor in charge. Keith and I will also be making our way to Hope Springs in the not-too-distant future. We'll be working with Peter on the projects he's lined up," Joshua explained.

"I promised these guys that if they came with me to Hope Springs, there'd be some nice, down-to-earth ladies for them to meet," Peter said, smiling. "Of course, I think one is already off the table. Macy is on Jake's radar, guys."

Jake set down the kitchen chair he had just picked up. "I don't know about that one, Peter."

"What's wrong with her?" asked Joshua. He picked up the chair Jake had just set down and put it in the truck. "Is she missing her teeth or something?"

Jake handed him the other chair to put in the truck. "No, nothing like that. Macy just doesn't seem too interested in me. And besides, she's my nurse. You know, conflict of interest and all."

"Jake, you and I both know Macy's interested in you," Peter argued. "Chandler told me so as well. She just cautioned you to take it slow with Macy."

"Well, can't go much slower than her not speaking to me," Jake stated. "But you're right. Rosie said the same thing as well."

"Chandler I know about, but who's Rosie?" asked Keith, taking the last piece of furniture to the truck.

"Rosie's my grandmother," answered Peter. "You'll get to meet her as well as all the other ladies of the Advice Quilting Bee."

Keith put the small table he was carrying in the truck for Joshua to pack. "The what?" he asked.

Jake laughed. "Don't worry, Keith. We'll fill you in on all of them at dinner." He looked around to make sure everything was out of the storage unit and proclaimed they were ready to go.

As they pulled up to Jake's house an hour later, Chandler stood on the front porch. "Hey, boys," she called out. "I thought you might need some nourishment before you started unloading, so I brought sweet tea from Rosie and pastries from the bakery."

Peter walked up the steps and gave his fiancé a big kiss. "Bless you!" he exclaimed. "Jake wasn't going to feed us anything!"

After Keith backed the truck up into the driveway, Peter introduced him and Joshua to Chandler. "Guys, this is the reason why I will never leave Hope Springs."

"Well, if there are more like Chandler here, then I may never leave either!" Keith said enthusiastically. "And thanks for the goodies!"

"My pleasure," Chandler answered. "I have to get back to the bakery, but I believe Andrea will have a catered lunch ready when you've finished unloading."

"Wow! Is this the kind of treatment every new resident of Hope Springs gets?" asked Joshua, taking a bite of the cinnamon roll.

"Nope, just the new town doctor," Jake teased. "You know, kind of like back in the olden days."

"Does that mean we can pay you with chickens and potatoes from our garden?" asked Chandler teasingly.

"You may pay me in cinnamon rolls," Jake answered after taking a bite of the still warm roll.

"Deal," Chandler said. "Well, I'll let you get back to work." She gave Peter one last kiss. "See you all later!" she said as she walked back toward town.

"Man, I could get used to this," Keith said, finishing his second roll and glass of sweet tea.

"Okay, guys," Jake urged, "let's finish this up."

For as long as it took to pack the truck, it only took about half that time to unload it. Jake directed where furniture and boxes needed to go. "The first thing I'll be setting up is the flat-screen TV. The Crusaders are on tonight, so I figured I'd put that on while I unpack everything else."

"Hey, that's all you need," Keith said, "TV, a comfy couch, and a stocked fridge. The rest can wait till you have a lady in your life."

"This coming from a guy who has the most organized bachelor kitchen I've ever seen," replied Joshua, laughing. "He even has his spices alphabetized!"

"Oh, but there's a method to my madness, young buck. What woman could resist a man who's also a gourmet chef," Keith explained.

Peter looked at Joshua. "Tell Jake how many dates you've gone out on in the last few months."

Jake looked at Joshua as he started to squirm and decided to help him out. "That's okay, buddy. I'm right there with you. Maybe things will look up for both of us in Hope Springs."

"It did for me," Peter proudly smiled.

Jake sure hoped his luck would be as good as Peter's. He was tired of living alone, eating alone, watching TV at night alone. He was just plain tired of being alone. He looked at the three men standing amidst the boxes and furniture in his living room. He was already best friends with Peter but was having fun hanging with Joshua and Keith, too. He wondered if the Hope Springs magic would rub off on all three of the single guys in the room. He sure hoped so.

The four men continued setting the furniture where Jake thought it would be best. Since the front of the home was one large room, they placed the sofa lengthwise in the middle, creating a living room on the left side and a dining room on the right. Unlike Chandler's cottage, which had the kitchen closed off in the back, the owners chose to make the right side of the cottage one long room. The dining room was open to the kitchen, giving the feel of an open L-shape. The bathroom and large master bedroom were on the left side of the home, and the second smaller bedroom was beyond that. A door going out from the kitchen led to a brick patio overlooking the backyard. Jake was looking forward to buying patio furniture to fill the space.

"I don't know about you guys, but I'm starved," Peter announced, looking at his watch. "Let's head up to the diner. Chandler texted and said Andrea was ready for us."

"Sounds good to me," Keith agreed. "Can we all go in one vehicle?"

Jake looked at him and laughed. "As the town doctor, I think we could use the exercise and walk."

"And besides," Peter chimed in, "it's only two blocks."

"Yeah, you can pretty much walk everywhere in Hope Springs in about twenty minutes," Jake answered.

"Alright then, lead the way," Joshua said, heading toward the door.

As the group headed down Main Street, Peter noticed a familiar group sitting on the benches across from the diner.

"Don't look now, but the Little Old Lady Network has spotted us," he informed his friends. He explained that the Little Old Lady Network was a subset of the Advice Quilting Bee and that they were this town's version of social media. "By the time lunch is over, the whole town will know we've been here and that there are two more good-looking guys in town. My guess is Myrtle, the ring leader, will have already picked out brides for the two of you by then," he explained to Joshua and Keith.

They both looked at him with shocked expressions. "You're kidding, right?" asked Joshua, incredulously. Then he looked at Keith and Jake. "He's kidding, right?"

Jake just smiled. "Don't think so. It's what they live for—fresh meat."

Keith opened his mouth to say something, but Joshua beat him to it. "Fresh meat?! Just what kind of town is this anyway?"

"The kind where everyone knows everyone, and also everyone's business," Peter answered. "You know, a small town. And you're gonna love it!" he said, slapping Joshua on the back.

Once they arrived at the diner, Jake opened the door to enter and was surprised to see the place packed! Apparently, this wasn't just lunch, but a "Welcome to Hope Springs, Dr. Grainger" party!

Chapter 9

Jake looked around the room and saw all the residents giving him a standing ovation. He had never experienced anything like it. Even the mayor was there, looking very official like he was going to award Jake the key to the city or something. He turned and looked at Peter standing behind him. "Is this for real? Did you get this type of reception?"

"Nope," Peter answered, shaking his head from side to side. "Of course, I haven't moved here yet, so maybe I will."

"Man, this is awesome!" Joshua practically shouted to be heard over the ovation. "Jake, what did you do to deserve all this?"

About that time, Mayor Thompson stepped forward and quieted the crowd. "Now everyone, please calm down so we can welcome our new town doctor properly. Dr. Grainger, it is with great privilege that I, the mayor of Hope Springs, welcome you to our town. It's been a long time since we've had a new doctor, and we're excited you've come to Hope Springs," Mayor Thompson declared. "As much as we loved Dr. Howard, we all know he was an old school doctor set in his ways. We're looking forward to some fresh ideas regarding the health and wellbeing of the citizens of Hope Springs. I hope you have some ideas to help us get healthy and stay healthy."

Jake was a bit taken aback by the mayor's request. He was sure he could come up with some healthy alternatives for the town's citizens, but not on the spur of the moment. Luckily for him, Peter bailed him out.

"Well, actually," Peter began, "Dr. Grainger has inquired about exercise facilities in Hope Springs."

By now, the Little Old Lady Network ladies had made their way across the street and were in the restaurant. "You could come and exercise with us at the church on Friday mornings, Dr. Grainger!" Myrtle shouted enthusiastically.

Jake smiled at the thought. "As much as I appreciate the invitation, Myrtle, I was thinking more along the lines of running or walking clubs."

"That's a wonderful idea," the mayor agreed. A few more folks shouted out ideas of their own to get the community moving and healthier.

All was going well until an older gentleman named Frank suggested closing the Sweet Stuff Bakery to get rid of temptation. "I don't think that will be necessary," Chandler stated diplomatically, and maybe a little emphatically. "If you think my sweets are too much of a temptation, don't keep coming in my shop every morning for breakfast, Frank!" That brought a chorus of cheers for Chandler's cinnamon rolls.

"Alright," Andrea spoke up, "let's get this party started by letting the guest of honor and the men who helped him move in go through the buffet line first. I will tell you, however, that you'll have to start your health kick tomorrow because nothing on this buffet is low-fat or low-cal!"

Jake hugged Andrea. "Bless you, because Peter and I have been telling Keith and Joshua all day about the fabulous fattening food you prepare. As the town doctor, I wholly support your menu." He turned to his new friends. "Keith and Joshua, let me introduce you to Andrea Porter, proprietor of the Hope Springs Diner, and one fabulous cook."

Joshua shook her hand. "Nice to meet you."

As Andrea stepped forward to shake Keith's hand, a little jolt went through her. She thought she felt Keith jump just a bit too. Or was it her imagination? "Thanks for doing all this for us," Keith said by way of introduction. "Everything looks delicious."

Andrea didn't see that Fran and Myrtle were over in the corner watching the exchange. Myrtle looked at Fran with a look Fran had seen far too often. "Oh no," Fran whispered, "you leave Andrea alone. We still haven't gotten Macy and Jake together."

Myrtle silenced her with a wave of her hand. "I know, but it's nice to know we have more in the pipeline."

Fran just shook her head from side to side. "Come on, let's get in line for the buffet."

Once Jake had his plate loaded with meatloaf, fried chicken, homemade mashed potatoes, green beans with bacon, and homemade applesauce, he made his way to a table for six. His moving buddies followed suit, leaving two chairs. One was taken by Chandler next to Peter. Chandler then motioned for Macy to sit in the last seat next to Jake. He was surprised when she sat down—and even more surprised when she spoke!

"Boy, Jake, I didn't get this kind of reception when I moved to town. You must be someone special!" Macy remarked, nudging him in the arm.

Jake didn't want to make a big deal out of the fact that Macy spoke directly to him, so he chose, instead, to introduce her to Joshua and Keith. "Guys, meet my nurse, Macy. If it hadn't been for her, I'd still be trying to figure out what mystery ailment had brought the ladies of the Little Old Lady Network to the medical center the other day."

Keith took a bite of meatloaf and almost sighed out loud. "Oh, yeah? What ailment?" he asked, between bites.

Macy smiled. "Dr. Grainger thought they might be suffering from food poisoning, although none of them had eaten the same thing."

Jake put down his fork. "But fortunately, Macy was familiar with the group and smelled a rat. It seemed they were only interested in me, and the thought of having to take a spoonful of castor oil to cure what ailed them was enough to have them running for the door."

Joshua turned up his nose. "Is that how a small-town doctor cures patients these days? Didn't you learn anything new in all those years of medical school?"

Jake started laughing and explained that there was no need to prescribe anything stronger since they weren't sick. "Macy's diagnosis and cure were spot on."

The conversation at the table soon turned to the development Peter's company was doing in Hope Springs and when Joshua and Keith would be making their way to town. If all went according to plan, they would be moving in the fall.

Of course, what this table didn't realize was that Myrtle and the Little Old Lady Network had situated themselves at a table directly behind them so they could hear everything that was said. Myrtle looked at Fran. "It's going to be an interesting fall in Hope Springs."

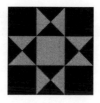

Chapter 10

Sunday morning, Macy was actually up in time to go to church. After the lunchtime party for Jake on Saturday afternoon, she and Jake were invited by Peter and Chandler to dinner at the winery to talk about wedding plans, Chandler had said. But she knew that wasn't the reason. Macy decided to go and be open-minded to whatever happened.

As it turned out, they all had a wonderful time. The food was excellent, the wine was delicious, and the atmosphere relaxing. They spent several hours on the deck overlooking the mountains watching the people come and go. There was even a wedding off to one side of the vast vineyard. With the setting sun as a backdrop, the happy couple pledged to love, honor, and cherish one another forever. Macy thought at the time that it was perhaps the most beautiful sight she'd ever seen. She even got a little teary-eyed. Of course, it could have been the three glasses of wine causing her to tear up so easily.

When they had finally arrived back at Chandler's, sometime after eleven, Macy was more than relaxed. And when Jake said he'd walk her home, she had to laugh. She wasn't sure if he realized she just lived across the street! But she let him walk her home. However, he had turned and started walking in the opposite direction. She remembered looking back at Chandler and seeing Chandler put her finger to her lips, telling her not to correct him. Macy just started letting him lead her around Hope Springs.

They walked across Main Street to the historic district. He commented on a few of the houses, saying it would be nice to live in one of them someday. She agreed, as long as ghosts didn't inhabit them. Jake looked at her as if to say she must be joking, but she made it clear that it was a possibility. Hope Springs was full of ghosts; she remembered telling him.

Eventually, they had walked back around to Main Street and continued across and down by the lake. Macy explained that this was one place where people claimed to see a couple walking hand in hand who had died decades earlier. She hadn't seen them, but others had. Jake told her he thought all this talk of ghosts was fascinating, but he wasn't too sure they existed.

Soon they were back at her place, and he was walking her to the door and unlocking it for her. She wasn't sure if she wanted him to kiss her or not, but she never had the option of deciding. She wasn't going to lie, she'd been a little disappointed when he didn't, but it was probably for the best. He just made sure she was safe inside and said he'd see her Monday morning.

Now, as she finished getting ready for church, Macy thought not kissing was definitely for the best. She had a much clearer head than she had had the night before and realized that would have been a colossal mistake. Just walking around town with Jake had been a big step for her. She wasn't ready for much more than that.

Macy looked at the clock on the built-in microwave above the stove and saw that it was time to leave. She quickly rinsed her empty coffee cup and placed it in the dishwasher. Macy stepped out onto her front porch, grabbing her purse and keys on the way out. Even though her house faced north and was shaded in the morning, she noted that the heat and humidity were back in full force. It was going to be another scorcher.

Chandler was coming out of her house at the same time, and as with most Sundays, the two walked to church together. A very excited Chandler practically shouted, "So, tell me everything that happened after you and Jake left last night!"

Macy took the time to hug her, giving her a moment to decide how to respond. "Well, as you saw last night, he took a wrong turn when walking me home."

"Yes, yes," Chandler confirmed excitedly, "Now quit stalling and tell me the details before we get to church and everyone else can hear."

"There isn't much to tell," Macy continued. "We walked around the historic district, and Jake commented on a few of the houses that might be fun to live in. I stated that I would only live in one if I were assured it wasn't haunted. He didn't believe me, so I told him about how haunted the town supposedly is. We continued our walk going down by the lake." She paused as a couple passed, going the opposite way on the sidewalk.

"Did you tell him about the ghost couple down by the lake?" Chandler interjected.

"Yes, I did. I told him I hadn't seen them, but others claim to have. I'm still not sure he's buying into it. Anyway, then we continued our walk back to my house."

"And?"

"And he walked me to my door, made sure I was safely inside, said he'd see me Monday and walked away."

"That's it!?" Chandler all but shouted. "No goodnight kiss?!"

Macy looked around to make sure no one else heard Chandler's loud remark. "No, and I wouldn't expect one," Macy whispered emphatically. "Personally, I think that would have been a huge mistake considering how much wine I'd consumed." Macy wasn't ready for such a step.

Chandler just stared at her in disbelief. Then, seeing the worried expression on Macy's face, she decided it probably had been for the best. If Jake had any hope at all with Macy, it was best to take it slow. "Well, I consider it a big step for you to go for a walk with Jake alone," she smiled, wrapping her arm around Macy's shoulder. By now, they had reached the steps of the church. "Let's go in and pray for another great week."

They took their usual seats, surrounded by the other members of the Advice Quilting Bee. Macy could feel their love and support wrap her in their imaginary quilt. She quietly sighed and settled in for the service.

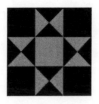

Chapter 11

Jake spent much of Sunday unpacking the myriad of boxes, taking up space in pretty much every room of his small rental. He had no idea how he'd fit all this stuff in his apartment in the city. It was smaller than his new home. Everywhere he looked, he saw boxes he'd yet to unpack. He could swear they were multiplying before his eyes.

As he worked in his den, unpacking what had to be the fifth box of medical books, Jake replayed the events of the previous night. He'd had such a great time with Macy, especially walking around his new hometown. Macy knew a lot about the place for someone who hadn't been here for more than a year, especially about the ghost stories. As a physician, the practical side of him knew he really shouldn't believe in ghosts, but his more romantic side thought it was a fascinating possibility. He'd have to ask Peter if he knew anything about them the next time that he saw him.

Continuing to recall the events of the evening, Jake also knew that he'd come close to kissing Macy at the end of the night. In reality, it was all he could do not to. Following the advice of Rosie, he decided it best if he continued to take things slow. If this relationship were meant to happen, then it would happen, fast or slow.

Jake had just finished the last of the boxes in his den when he heard a knock at the front door. Looking at his watch, he saw it was after noon. He opened the door to find

Myrtle standing on his front porch. "Hello, Myrtle," he greeted her with a smile. "How did I get so lucky as to have such a lovely visitor as yourself?"

He could tell he caught her off guard with the compliment. "Well, I uh," Myrtle stammered.

"Won't you come in?" Jake said, stepping aside for her to enter. "Now, please excuse the massive amount of boxes. I'm still in the process of unpacking." He noticed Myrtle was dressed more subdued than her usual florescent, bright, flowery garb. "Did you just come from church?" he asked.

"Why, yes, Dr. Grainger," she answered. She looked him up and down, making Jake feel a little underdressed in his red Crusaders t-shirt and khaki cargo shorts. "And you were missed. Do you not go to church?" Her tone made him feel like a child who'd been caught by the nuns skipping mass.

Jake smiled. "I haven't been in a while. With my schedule, it was tough for me to attend on Sundays. But I do believe it will be easier here in Hope Springs."

Myrtle nodded her head, agreed with him, and walked into the living room to look around. Jake was sure she was making a mental picture to report back to the Little Old Lady Network. "This is very nice," she said, continuing her perusal of the space. "The owners have done a wonderful job restoring the home. Other than opening up the wall between the dining room and kitchen, it's not much different than when it was built."

That took Jake a little by surprise. "Myrtle, this wasn't your house, was it?" That would have been weird.

Myrtle patted Jake on the arm and smiled. "Oh no, dear. But our good friends, the Shaw family, lived here for many years."

"Oh, did they move elsewhere?"

Myrtle looked at him with a wry smile. "You could say that. The children moved on to other places around the country, but the parents remained here until they passed away about four years ago. The house sat vacant for almost two years until the current owners bought it and began the restoration process."

"Oh," Jake commented. "How did they die?"

"The Shaws were both in their eighties and died within a month of each other. He passed first of a heart attack, and she a month later from a broken heart," Myrtle explained. "You haven't seen them around yet, have you?" she asked, waving her hands around the room.

"What?!" Jake asked, swearing he hadn't heard her right.

"Didn't Roger or the owners tell you about the ghosts?" Myrtle asked, matter-of-factly, noting the surprised look on Jake's face.

"Do I look like I know anything about ghosts in my home?!" Jake exclaimed.

Myrtle continued walking into the kitchen. "I can't believe they didn't tell you, Jake."

"What were they supposed to tell me?" he asked, following her into the kitchen. "I'm suddenly very thirsty, Myrtle. Can I get you something to drink?" he asked as he got himself a beer from the fridge.

76

Myrtle chuckled. "Beer might be a little strong for me at this time of day. However, something non-alcoholic would be nice."

Jake took his time getting her a bottle of water from the refrigerator, twisting the cap off, and handing it to her. "I'd offer you a glass, but I haven't finished unpacking the kitchen yet." Then, "I think I need to sit down." He motioned for her to join him at the kitchen table.

Myrtle took a big sip of the cool water, putting the bottle on the table. "Apparently, there had been apparitions of Maggie and Horace Shaw spotted by the construction workers. They'd also reported tools being moved and floors having been swept."

Jake took a swig of his beer. "Do you mean to tell me that I have ghosts in my home who *clean*?" he asked, still not believing what he was hearing. Seeing them down by the lake was one thing, but this was a bit too much!

Myrtle smiled at the question. "Maggie was quite the housekeeper in her day. I don't think a speck of dust was allowed to land anywhere in her home."

Jake took another swig, relishing the way the cold liquid went down. "I'm not sure if I believe all this," he said skeptically. "But if I do notice anything, I'll let you know so you can report back to the network." Saying Little Old Lady Network just took too much effort, so Jake took it upon himself to shorten the moniker.

Myrtle nodded her head and toasted his beer with her water. "Alright, deal."

Jake finally realized that ghosts might not have been Myrtle's reason for this impromptu visit. "So, what's the real reason for this unexpected visit?"

"Well," Myrtle began, "I was just wondering what you're going to do about Macy?"

Jake looked at her quizzically. "I'm not sure what you mean."

"Oh, come on now, Jake. We both know you're interested in her as more than just your nurse. And I happen to know you were both out walking all over town last night on a romantic moonlit stroll." Myrtle frustratingly replayed the previous night's events.

"Romantic moonlit stroll?" asked Jake, somewhat shocked Myrtle knew the details of their night. *Of course, Myrtle would know the details,* he thought. Probably a good thing he hadn't kissed Macy goodnight.

Myrtle just smiled her sheepish smile.

"I wouldn't call it that," Jake said. "It was more like two friends enjoying a nice evening. I would appreciate it if you wouldn't make it more than that."

Myrtle took a drink of her water before answering. "Look, Jake, we all know Macy is hiding something from her past, and none of us wants her to get hurt. I'm just here to make sure you understand and want the same thing."

Jake was more than a little annoyed with Myrtle at the moment. "Are you here to warn me not to hurt Macy?"

"Yes," Myrtle answered, matter-of-factly.

"Myrtle, as I'm sure you remember, Macy is also my employee. The last thing I would do is hurt anyone for my own personal pleasure. If that's what you think, then this conversation is over."

"Oh, my, I'm afraid you have misunderstood my intentions," Myrtle said worriedly.

Then Jake figured out just why Myrtle was visiting him. "No, I think I understood pretty well. Myrtle, you're fishing for information that I'm not at liberty to provide," Jake explained. "If you want to know about Macy's past, maybe you should ask her, not me."

Myrtle finished her water and got up from the table. Looking around and not seeing a trash can or recycling bin, she left the empty bottle on the table. "Thank you for the water and conversation. It seems we both want the same thing, and that's all that matters."

As Jake walked Myrtle to the door, he agreed, "If somehow Macy and I do end up having more than a working relationship, I'd like to take it slow. And, to handle it on my terms."

"Duly noted," Myrtle acknowledged. She hugged him before leaving. "Watch out for Maggie and Horace!" was her parting shot.

Jake closed the door and turned around, surveying the living room, dining room, and kitchen. "Maggie, if you want to help me clean, then have at it," he said to the empty space, with a smile on his face. He shook his head and got back to work.

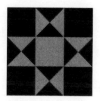

Chapter 12

"Okay, Rosie, what's for dinner tonight?" Myrtle asked on Thursday evening as she walked into Rosie's Quilting Emporium for the weekly Advice Quilting Bee meeting.

"Tonight, we're having a taco salad with cornbread," Rosie answered as she helped Ruth Garten pick out fabric for her new grandson. "Ruth, I think this truck fabric will be perfect for the border."

"I agree," Ruth replied. "The blue background on the allover print coordinates nicely with the other fabrics we chose for the truck blocks. You know, Jimmy played with these same kinds of trucks in our yard forever when he was a child. I couldn't keep that boy clean!"

"Then this is the one you should get." Rosie took the bolt to the cutting table. "How much would you like?"

Ruth looked at the fabric laid out on the table. "Luckily, it's not a directional print, and they put the trucks going all different directions. I think a yard should do."

Rosie measured and cut a little over a yard. She always made sure her customers had a little extra in case they decided to prewash their fabrics. Some quilters swore by prewashing, and others didn't. Fabrics these days weren't as prone to shrinkage as in the past, but she always made sure her customers had enough fabric to complete their project.

"Do you need anything else, dear?" Rosie asked as she finished writing up the ticket.

"I think that's all I need," Ruth said, looking around. "Of course, I'll have to come back when I have more time because it seems you always have something new."

"You are welcome to come in and browse anytime," Rosie answered, taking Ruth's fabrics to the register where Mary Ann was waiting to ring up the sale. "Thank you so much for stopping by, and please bring in the completed quilt so we can see your beautiful work."

"I'll do that," Ruth said, smiling.

Once Mary Ann completed the sale and walked Ruth to the door, she and Rosie got to work closing up for the evening.

"Did you both realize that no one told Jake about Maggie and Horace?" Myrtle asked as she helped straighten the rows of fabric.

"Oh, Myrtle, you didn't fill his head with that nonsense, did you?" Mary Ann admonished. "Honestly, I know that supposedly Robert saw those ghosts in the field when he was growing up, but I don't believe it. What do you think, Rosie?"

"It's not for me to say whether they exist or not, but remember you had that note from Chandler's father at the winery." Rosie reminded Mary Ann about the waiter who had advised Chandler to marry Peter.

"That's right," Myrtle agreed. "Didn't you say you had two waiters that night, and one was named Steven?"

"Yes, that's true. And when I asked our original waiter where Steven was, he told us there was no one named Steven. And instead of a bill, I got the note for Chandler. But that guy wasn't a ghost in the literal sense. He actually gave us our order, so I'm not sure that qualifies," Mary Ann concluded. She finished the night deposit from the register and closed it up. "I'm going to take this over to the bank and drop it off. You two can keep carrying on about ghosts, but I'm going to focus on the living." She left Rosie and Myrtle to finish straightening up.

A few minutes later, Mary Ann returned to see that most of the members of the Advice Quilting Bee were already present. "Howdy, everybody," she greeted them.

"Hi, Mary Ann," Fran said first. "Myrtle tells us she has informed Jake about Maggie and Horace."

Mary Ann just rolled her eyes and began getting a plate of food. "Macy, has Dr. Grainger mentioned anything to you and the others at the medical center about Maggie and Horace?"

Macy smiled and put some salad on her plate. "No, not yet. But do you really think he would? Imagine the town doctor confessing to seeing ghosts! That could be quite the scandal."

"Oh, heavens, yes," Fran agreed, chuckling. "We certainly don't need the citizens thinking our doctor is crazy!" She put some chips and salsa on her plate and took a seat to have her dinner. "We were busy at the mercantile today, and I didn't have time to eat. I'm starved!"

"I hear ya," agreed Macy, plopping down in the seat next to Fran. "We're in the middle of school physical season, and we were swamped."

Myrtle took the opening she had been waiting for. "So, Macy, how are things going with Dr. Grainger?"

Macy knew exactly what Myrtle meant but chose to go in a different direction. "Things are going great," she answered, smiling.

"Really?" Myrtle asked incredulously. "Any details you want to share?"

"Myrtle! I don't think we need to hear the details!" Fran scolded.

"Oh, no, it's okay," Macy remarked, smiling. "Dr. Grainger is getting along wonderfully with all the patients and the staff."

Fran raised her glass to Macy. "Good answer."

"Not what I wanted to hear," Myrtle grumbled.

"What do you expect her to say?" Rosie asked. "That he doesn't get along with anyone?"

"I wasn't talking about Dr. Grainger; I was talking about Jake," Myrtle stubbornly answered. "Tell us about your relationship with Jake."

"Now, Myrtle, leave the poor girl alone," Candy, who hardly contributes to the conversations, admonished. "She doesn't have to tell you everything. Can't a girl have some secrets?"

Myrtle opened her mouth to tell her daughter-in-law to mind her own business and then thought better of it. Candy never offered up her thoughts or opinions when they all got together, and she didn't want to discourage her from doing so in the future.

"Yeah, Myrtle," Andrea agreed with Candy. "You badgered poor Chandler to death about her relationship with Peter. Perhaps Macy doesn't want to tell us every little detail."

"That's true, Myrtle," Chandler commented. "There were times I didn't want to come on Thursdays because I was afraid that I was going to be grilled."

Myrtle opened her mouth to say it wasn't true but then thought better of it. She decided a little humility was in order. "You all know we just have your best interests at heart, right?" she asked the younger members of the group. "We, and by that, I mean Rosie, Fran, and myself feel it is our duty to make sure you have every happiness you deserve. We didn't have a group like this to go to for advice about our love lives. We want to be here for you."

Macy looked around at the group. She was the first to speak. "We appreciate all the advice you ladies give us. And for me, this is the closest I'll ever get to a family."

Rosie noted that this was the first time Macy had spoken about family or lack thereof. Maybe she was starting to open up. "You know we're here for you whenever you need us."

"We know," Chandler answered for the younger members. "And we are grateful for all of you." Chandler also noticed that Macy had let a little information slip. This was something she hadn't even told her. Chandler thought it was about time for a little wine and conversation on the porch later.

"Well, I think dinner hour is over," Mary Ann said. "Come on, ladies, we've got work to do." Everyone helped clean up from dinner and took their place around the quilting frame.

"Two more weeks, and we should have this done," Rosie announced to the group. "We want to give Mary Ann time to bind it before we present it to Katrina."

"I've been watching the progress on the park and the new construction," Hillary remarked, finishing threading her needle. "Jack thinks Peter's revitalization plan is going to bring new people to the town."

Andrea agreed. "And from what I hear, the two men who helped get Jake moved in are planning on moving here as well. Isn't that right, Chandler?"

Chandler finished the stitch she was making before replying. "Sounds like it. Both Joshua and Keith are going to look at moving here in the next couple of months."

"How old do you think those two are?" asked Myrtle, taking off her reading glasses. From her perspective, more single men in town meant a bigger dating pool for the single ladies.

Chandler thought for a moment. "Um, I guess Joshua would be in his mid-twenties and Keith in his forties, maybe. Why?"

"Just wondering," Myrtle responded, putting her glasses back on.

"Too young for you, Myrtle," Fran told her friend.

Myrtle looked at her friend over her reading glasses. "And too young for you as well."

The conversation turned toward the Labor Day celebration that was to be in a couple of weeks. Everyone was so excited because they would have a concert from a local country band this year in the new gazebo/bandstand that Peter was building. There was going to be a massive potluck picnic, with games for everyone. The evening would end with a firework display to mark the official end of summer.

Macy continued working on her section of the quilt, feeling more confident with every stitch. She was finally getting the hang of hand quilting, even if she wasn't so confident in her personal life. She hadn't been sure if she'd ever be ready to date again. That little bit of time she had spent with Jake on Saturday night, however, made her feel like maybe she was. But then Monday morning had come around, and she'd been back to being her shy self around him.

Of course, she didn't think he even noticed her. He hadn't said more than two words to her this whole week unless it had been to talk about a patient. She wasn't sure what she had expected when they saw each other on Monday morning, but it certainly wasn't that he wouldn't acknowledge her at all! Maybe she had read way too much into their evening stroll.

Before Macy knew it, everyone was packing up to go home. Somehow an entire hour had gone by, and she didn't even remember if she had participated in the conversation!

"Come on, Macy." Chandler put her arm around her. "I'll walk you home."

"Chandler, I do hope you aren't going to walk her home the same route that Jake took with her the other night?" Myrtle said snidely.

"We might. It's a nice night, and we need the exercise," Chandler answered as she practically pushed Macy out the door. "Goodnight, ladies!"

Macy started laughing as she practically fell out onto the sidewalk. "Chandler! If someone were watching, they would swear I was drunk!"

"No worries." Chandler began walking toward their street. "Anyone who would care is still in Rosie's."

Chapter 13

Jake woke up early Friday morning feeling restless. Since he didn't have to be at the medical center until nine o'clock, he had time for a good long run. After dressing in his blue and white college running shorts and tank top, Jake carried his shoes out to the front porch. It was a little after seven in the morning, and already the August heat was stifling.

He sat on the top step, pressed the button on his GPS watch to find the signal so it could map his route, and proceeded to lace up his shoes. Since this was his first time running in his new neighborhood, he had no idea how far to go to get in a ten-mile run.

After doing a few stretches, Jake started running. He never ran with headphones, choosing to listen to the sounds around him instead. When he'd lived in the city, it had been safer to run without headphones, so he was used to it.

As he ran north toward the high school, Jake could hear whistles blowing and men yelling. *Ah, early morning football practice*, he surmised. Jake remembered it all too well from when he played in high school. Lord knows how he hated two-a-days. His team would practice from eight o'clock until noon and then break for lunch until two. Then they'd practice until six or seven in the evening. He would come home so exhausted every night that he could barely keep his eyes open to eat his dinner. But in the end, his team had gone to the state championship all four years he'd been on the team, so it had all been worth it.

Jake thought he'd see if the track was available to rack up some extra mileage. As he entered the stadium, he saw one of the assistant coaches who had brought his infant son in earlier in the week for an ear infection.

"Hi, John, how is little Johnny doing?" Jake asked as he got close enough for the coach to hear him.

John turned in the direction of the question. "Hey, doc! Johnny is doing much better, and we're getting more sleep again," he answered, laughing. "What brings you out this way?"

"Good to hear," Jake acknowledged. "I was wondering if it would be okay to use the track during practice. Hope Springs isn't that big, and I'd like to get a run in of about ten miles before work."

"Sure, the track's open all day," John told him. "The team won't need it."

"This brings back a lot of memories from when I was in high school," Jake said.

"Oh yeah?" John asked. "What position did you play?"

"I was a linebacker all four years," Jake answered. "But I hated two-a-days with a passion!"

John started laughing. "Yeah, I don't think anyone likes them. But it's a necessary evil of the sport."

"Yep," Jake agreed. "Well, I'd better get going if I'm going to get my run in and have time to shower before work. I don't think my staff would like me very much if I didn't!"

John chuckled. "Have a good run."

Jake turned and started running around the track. His mind went back over the past week. They had been so busy at the medical center with back-to-school physicals and sick patients that he hadn't had much time alone with Macy, let alone time to talk to her. They'd had a good time Saturday night walking around town, but like he told Myrtle, he wanted to take things slow. He wouldn't be pressured to do otherwise. As far as he was concerned, he would wait for Macy to make the next move. There was nothing wrong with letting things develop naturally.

Jake was so deep in thought that he didn't hear John yelling for him on his fourth time around the track.

"Doc! Doc!" John yelled.

Jake turned toward the field to see a crowd gathering. He ran toward them, and the group parted for him to see a player lying on the ground, not moving. He bent down and first checked to see if he was breathing. Grateful to know that he was, he realized that he was out cold. "What happened?" he asked no one in particular.

John was quick to tell him that they were running a play. "And Cody just dropped like a rock." Another coach ran up and said they had just called nine-one-one. Off in the distance, the fire alarm sounded, so Jake knew help would be on the way.

"Someone help me get his helmet and shoes off," Jake ordered. "He may be suffering from heat exhaustion."

A couple of other coaches did as he asked. At about that time, Cody regained consciousness. He tried to sit up, but Jake told him to stay put until he could examine him. "Since

I don't have any equipment with me," he explained, "we'll have to wait until the ambulance arrives." The boy did as he was told.

Soon, Ben Freeman, the fire chief, and Candy's husband arrived with the ambulance, and Jake was able to ascertain that Cody could be moved to the gurney for transport to the medical center. "I want to do a full work up there," he told the coaches. "Will someone notify his parents so they can meet me there?"

He heard an assistant coach say that they had already done so. The parents were on their way to the field, but he would direct them to the medical center.

Once Ben and the paramedics were loading Cody into the waiting ambulance, Jake turned to John and the other coaches. "Who is the athletic trainer on duty when you're practicing? I just realized that I hadn't seen any medical personnel."

The head coach, Coach Franks, spoke up, "We don't have it in the school budget to have an athletic trainer just for our school. We share one with Cromwell High about twenty miles from here, and they are only at our school on Tuesdays and Thursdays. The rest of the time, we're on our own."

Jake thought for a minute. "I'm not comfortable with that. There should be someone on-site during practice. Send me the practice schedule for all your athletic teams, and I'll see what I can do. I may not be able to cover every sport all the time, but I should be able to do something."

"You realize we can't pay you with anything but game tickets, right?" Coach Franks asked, clearly surprised Jake wanted to do this.

"The way I see it is either we make sure someone is monitoring things on the practice field, or I'll be seeing them in the medical center. I'd rather not have it come to that if I can help it." Jake went on to explain, "I may be able to see if any of the colleges need to place sports medicine interns, as well. I remember a few of my college classmates did that."

Coach Franks got a smile on his face for the first time since Cody hit the ground. "Son, if you can do that, we'd sure appreciate it. I lay awake at night worrying about what would happen if one of our players got seriously injured, or worse, and we couldn't treat them." He reached out to shake Jake's hand.

"I'm just glad I was here this morning, Coach," Jake said, shaking the coach's hand. "Now, get that practice schedule over to me as soon as you can. I'm going to go treat Cody and speak with his parents. In the meantime, please make sure these kids are well hydrated and get plenty of rest breaks out of the sun."

"You bet," Coach Franks answered.

Jake quickly ran to the medical center, fortunately only a few blocks from the high school. When he arrived, he saw that Macy had already beaten him there and was helping to get Cody situated in the examining room.

"How did you know to come?" Jake asked her, clearly surprised she was there.

"I was at the diner having breakfast with Chandler when we heard the emergency sirens. Andrea has a scanner, and we heard everything. Figured you'd need help, so here I am," Macy explained, hooking Cody up to the blood pressure monitor.

Jake did a thorough exam of Cody and came to the same conclusion he had on the field. After Cody informed him that he'd eaten a whole pizza on a dare the night before and hadn't had anything to drink except sodas, the sodium intake had dehydrated him.

Macy brought Cody's parents back to the exam room so Jake could talk to all three of them. "It seems our star receiver decided to overload his system with pizza and soda last night and hadn't properly hydrated before practice. Everything else looks good, but he's going to have to hydrate properly from now on."

Cody's parents were relieved. "Thank goodness that's all it is," his mom said. "We'll keep an eye on all that from now on, Dr. Grainger."

Jake turned to Cody. "Does the athletic trainer do any type of training program with you guys before the season so you know what to do and the proper nutrition you need?"

Cody got a guilty look on his face. "Yeah, there was something. But honestly, doc, I'm not sure how many of us actually listen to it. It's the same day as the drug and steroid speech we get every year."

Jake understood. He remembered the same type of meeting from when he was in high school. "Well, I'm going to talk to Coach Franks to see if maybe I can come out to talk to the team. Maybe you'll listen to me."

"We might," Cody answered, looking down at his hands. "Can I go back to practice now?" he begged.

"I want Nurse Greenburg to check your vitals one more time. If everything looks good, you're cleared to go back to practice. But only if you hydrate." Jake motioned for Macy to come out into the hall.

Macy followed and finally noticed that Jake was not dressed for work. And, boy, did he look good! She had never seen him in shorts and such a tight shirt before. *Trouble,* Macy thought, *nothing but trouble.*

"As you can see, I'm not quite ready for work," Jake said, stating the obvious. "I realize it's close to nine o'clock, but I need to go get cleaned up."

Macy smiled. "You don't look much like a doctor dressed like that. I checked the schedule and our first patient isn't until nine-thirty, so you have time."

"Great," Jake said, breathing a sigh of relief. "If you don't mind, check Cody's vitals one more time, and if everything's still okay, he's free to go back to practice."

"I'll take care of it," Macy assured him, smiling. "Now you go home and don't come back until you smell better and look more like a doctor."

Jake just had to ask, "If I don't look like a doctor, just what do I look like?"

Macy chose not to take the bait, choosing instead to give him a huge smile and a wink and shoo him out the door.

As Macy watched Jake run back toward his house, she couldn't help but notice he was probably the most handsome man she had ever met. Did she want a relationship with him? She wasn't sure and didn't know how to find the answer. She then remembered Cody and his parents waiting for her and turned back toward the exam room.

"Macy, that new doctor is one fine-looking gentleman," Cody's mom stated. "And he sure was looking at you."

94

Macy chose to ignore the comment. "Okay, Cody, let's get you out of here." She proceeded to check his vital signs and declare him fit for practice.

As Cody hopped up out of bed, chugging the sports drink his dad had gone to the mercantile to get for him, his mom once again whispered to Macy, "Think about it, Macy. They don't come along in Hope Springs like that very often."

Macy just smiled and escorted them out the door. "Take care of yourself, Cody."

"Yes, ma'am," he shouted as he ran back toward the school.

Macy watched as his parents walked back to their car. Cody's mom was right. They didn't have too many like Jake in Hope Springs. That seemed to be a reoccurring theme in the town.

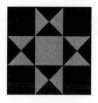

Chapter 14

Saturday morning dawned bright and sunny. Macy loved the weekend because she could sleep in. Even with shades on her bedroom window, the rising sun still peaked through the side and shone brightly. Macy stretched and rubbed the sleep from her eyes. Looking at the clock across the room, she saw that it was only six-thirty.

"Aw, man, I thought it was at least eight," she complained to no one in particular. Macy pushed back the covers and got out of bed, straightening her PJ capris and sleeveless top. She fluffed her hair and pushed it back from her face. Walking down the hall to the kitchen, she went about making a pot of coffee. While waiting for it to brew, Macy walked to her front window to see if there was any movement from Chandler's house.

Noting the front shades were open, she surmised that Chandler was probably up and already at the bakery. Saturday was always their busiest day because people like Macy didn't feel like having breakfast at home. Sweets from Sweet Stuff Bakery were always better than cereal at home.

Macy was just getting ready to turn around when another movement caught her eye. Her house was positioned so that she could see the kitchen window of Jake's rental perfectly. A small elderly woman was sweeping his kitchen floor. "Jake hired a cleaning lady already?" she questioned out loud. "And he has her working at six-thirty on a Saturday morning?! How cruel!" But just as quickly as she saw her, the woman was gone.

Soon Macy saw Jake standing at the kitchen window. She could tell he was doing something at the kitchen sink. Macy watched for another minute, feeling a little guilty for staring. She turned and went back to her kitchen to pour herself some coffee. Then she stopped dead in her tracks as she remembered hearing stories of how the spirits of the previous owners still inhabited his cottage. *Did I just see the ghost of Maggie sweeping Jake's floor?* Macy wondered. She was going to have to ask Jake if he had indeed hired a housekeeper.

Looking in her cupboard, Macy didn't want to have cereal for breakfast, so she decided to see if Gretchen's cinnamon rolls were ready at the bakery yet. *Yeah, two days in a row, but I don't care,* she argued with herself.

After showering, making her bed, and rinsing her cup in the sink, Macy headed out in search of breakfast. She had decided to dress in a pair of navy shorts, with a pink and white striped flowy tank top and pink sandals. It was nice on the weekends not to have to wear scrubs. After grabbing her purse and keys, she walked out into the sauna that was August in Hope Springs. She had chosen to put her long, red hair in a ponytail and was glad she did. *Why did I even bother with a shower?* she thought, sighing.

Macy walked a couple of blocks to Main Street and saw that Peter and his crew were already hard at work on the gazebo/bandstand in the park. As she stood at the corner of Spring and Main waiting for the light to change, Macy saw that Chandler was talking to Peter. Once the light changed, she made her way across and over to the park.

"Good morning!" Macy shouted to be heard above the construction noise. "Getting an early start, I see."

"Yeah," Peter acknowledged, wiping his forehead with his sleeve. "With the August heat, we want to get as much done as early as possible. Counting today, we only have two more Saturdays until the Labor Day festivities."

"The mayor is pushing for a big, grand ceremony where he can puff up his chest and make a speech about how his revitalization project is saving the town," Chandler said, rolling her eyes.

"Well, I guess that is part of his job," Macy remarked. Her stomach let out a growl loud enough for the whole town to hear. "I'm in search of cinnamon rolls. Do you think Gretchen has any yet?"

Chandler laughed. "I know for a fact she does. We had a batch ready early this morning for me to deliver to the men. We also have coffee ready." She turned to Peter, "I'll leave you to sweat in this heat. Macy and I are going back to the air-conditioned bakery." She kissed him and told him she'd see what she could do about bringing them lunch later.

"Do you think Andrea will have any of her world-famous chicken salad sandwiches available?" Peter asked.

"I think that could be arranged. How about noon?"

"Sounds good," Peter confirmed.

As Peter watched Chandler and Macy walk toward the bakery, he thought about how lucky he was and how much his life had changed in a short few months. He had initially come to Hope Springs to bid on a redevelopment project that would mean demolishing many historic buildings in the town. But after quickly learning from his Grandmother Rosie that the residents would never go for that, he set out to develop a new plan. In the process, he had fallen in love with the town baker and had asked her to marry him. Now he couldn't wait to make her his wife in this very gazebo in November, and make Hope Springs his new hometown. Life was good.

Chandler and Macy entered the bakery to the smell of fresh cinnamon rolls, coffee, bread, and all the other goodies that Gretchen and Luann had been busy preparing for the day. Macy's stomach let out another tremendous growl.

"Wow!" exclaimed Luann, from behind the counter. "I could hear that clear over here. Let's get you some breakfast before you faint." She put a fresh cinnamon roll on a plate and handed it over the counter to Macy.

"Thanks, I don't think I could have gone another minute," Macy said, gratefully taking the plate from Luann. "Between the heat and hunger, I was getting weak." She placed her free hand over her forehead, feigning weakness. "I'll help myself to a cup of coffee. Put it all on my tab."

Chandler laughed. "You do realize your tab is just imaginary, don't you?"

"Of course," Macy smiled, shrugging her shoulders while pouring her coffee. "But since we don't have a bar in town, it sounds cooler if I have a tab here."

"Why is it that we don't have a bar in Hope Springs?" Gretchen asked while taking cookies off a sheet fresh from the oven. "I wouldn't mind going for a drink after work."

Chandler's expression turned thoughtful, "You know, I don't remember us ever having a bar in Hope Springs. Maybe we should bring it up at our next Advice Quilting Bee. I do remember stories of Myrtle working in one back in the day. I wonder if some of the older members know what happened."

"Maybe there was some huge drunken scandal many years ago that caused Hope Springs to become dry," Luann surmised excitedly.

"Wouldn't that be interesting," Macy agreed as she and Chandler sat down at one of the tables by the window. Looking out across the street, they all saw Jake out for his morning run.

"Man, he's even better looking in exercise clothes," Luann said dreamily. "Macy, you are one lucky lady."

Macy dropped her fork and looked at Luann, "Me? What makes you think anything is going on between us?"

"Still in denial?" Gretchen asked as she slid a tray of peanut butter cookies into the display case.

"There's nothing to deny!" Macy protested as the door opened and two high school girls came in.

"Oh, look, Penny, they still have cinnamon rolls!" one of them exclaimed to the other. Turning to Luann, she asked, "Can we have six to go? And also six cheese Danishes?"

"Sure thing," Luann answered. "What are you up to today, girls?" she asked as she put their order together.

The one named Penny answered, "Oh, we have cheerleading practice today. As captains, we decided to bring goodies for the other girls."

"Oh, look," the other one said to Penny, "there goes Dr. Grainger. He's so cute!"

"I know," Penny sighed, also turning to look out the window. "My mom said that Cody's mom told her he has the hots for his nurse."

Macy almost choked on her coffee but gave Chandler a look that said, *don't say a word.*

"Bummer," the other cheerleader remarked. "Lucky her."

Luann decided to interrupt their conversation. "Here you go, girls. That'll be twelve dollars." After taking their money, she said, "Now run along back to practice."

"Thanks so much," Penny said cheerfully.

After they left, no one was sure what to say. Gretchen chose to break the silence. "So Dr. Grainger has the hots for his nurse? Let's see, well, Mary is in her sixties, so it couldn't possibly be her." She turned to Luann. "Who could it possibly be?" she asked, tapping her finger to her lips as if trying to figure it out.

"I don't know," Luann answered innocently. "But apparently to the high school cheerleading squad, she is 'lucky'."

Macy looked disgustedly at both of them. "Oh, honestly. Now I'm gossip for the high school moms?! It was bad enough when it was just the Little Old Lady Network!"

"Well," Chandler began, "I'm sure before sundown, they will have all met at the grocery store to compare notes. It's clear that Cody's mom saw something yesterday in the medical center that made her conclude that Jake has the 'hots' for you." She smiled as she got up to take Macy's cup and refill it. "You may want to lay low in here for a while.

Wouldn't want people to see you and Jake on the streets of the town at the same time."

"Very funny," Macy remarked sarcastically. "But I see that you're about to get busy, so I'll just sit here and enjoy my coffee while you work like a crazy woman."

They looked out the window to see several cars parked out front, as well as people walking up the sidewalk. Chandler turned to her employees. "Fun's over. Let the madness begin!"

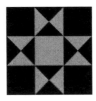

Chapter 15

Macy sat enjoying her coffee, watching the parade of people come in and out of the bakery, and her three friends working like madwomen for about half an hour. Since she was out of coffee, she decided it was time to head back home. She had some cleaning and laundry to do. She waved goodbye over the crowd of people and headed out the door.

But instead of heading home, Macy found herself going into Hillary's consignment shop instead.

"Hey, Macy!" Hillary greeted her from behind the counter. "Looking for anything in particular?"

"No, just browsing, if you don't mind," Macy remarked.

"Take your time and let me know if you need any help," Hillary answered as she finished up with another customer.

Macy went to the dress rack to see if anything caught her eye. She wasn't sure if she needed anything, but then again, it had been a long time since she'd bought something new. Not that there was anything "new" in the consignment shop, but it would be new to her. She was admiring a flowing maxi dress with a blue background and soft yellow flowers when Hillary came to check on her.

"That one would be beautiful on you," Hillary told her. "I'll put it in a dressing room for you. Keep looking to see if you see any others."

Macy continued browsing and found two more dresses, three pairs of palazzo pants, and three tops. "I just came in to browse," she commented to Hillary as she went into the dressing room.

Hillary hung the garments in the room for her. "Happens all the time." She left Macy to begin trying on garments.

As Macy was admiring herself in the full-length mirror, she heard Myrtle and Mabel enter the shop. She wanted to look at herself in the three-way mirror set up outside the room but didn't feel like getting their unsolicited opinions.

"Hi, ladies," Hillary greeted them. "Myrtle, I have a new selection you just have to see."

"Oh, great!" Myrtle exclaimed. "You know, we saw Dr. Grainger out running today," she heard Myrtle say. "We just have to get him and Macy together."

"Why is that?" Hillary asked, knowing Macy could hear every word. Macy was glad Hillary didn't tell them she was in the shop.

"Because they would be perfect for each other," Myrtle explained. "I don't know what Macy has against him, but she's just going to have to get over it."

"You know, maybe you should just let things happen naturally," Mabel advised. Macy was surprised Mabel spoke up, seeing as how she usually did whatever Myrtle told her to do.

"Naturally?!" Myrtle practically shouted. "If we let things happen naturally in this town, none of these young women would ever get married. They need us to help things along."

"I suppose you're right," Mabel acquiesced. *Darn it!* Macy thought. *Mabel, you were so close to having a backbone!*

Macy decided it was time to emerge from the dressing room. She wanted to see what she looked like in the three-way mirror. "Hillary, what do you think of this one?" she announced as she went to stand in front of the mirror.

Hillary got a big smile on her face. "Oh, Macy, that one is lovely!" She came over and mouthed, "great move". Hillary knew precisely what Macy was doing.

Macy turned to Myrtle and Mabel. "Since you all seem to have opinions for everything else in my life, what do you think of this dress?" She spun around so they could see it from all sides.

Myrtle got the usual scowl on her face, but Mabel spoke, "You look lovely, dear. Doesn't she, Myrtle?"

"Yes," Myrtle reluctantly agreed. "Will you be wearing it on a date with Jake?"

Macy just smiled, told Hillary she'd take the blue dress, and went back into the dressing room to try on more garments. She wasn't about to answer that question.

Mabel looked at Myrtle. "Does that mean she has a date with Jake or not?"

"Oh, shut up, Mabel," Myrtle scolded as she marched toward the door.

"Myrtle, what about the new clothes I was going to show you!" Hillary practically shouted.

"Maybe some other time," Myrtle replied. "I'm not getting a lot of respect in here today."

After Hillary watched them walk out the front door, she ran to the dressing room. "Way to go, Macy! You left them hanging!"

Macy came out of the dressing room wearing purple floral palazzo pants and a lavender top. "Can you believe them?! Even if I were going on a date with Jake, I wouldn't tell them. And for Myrtle to say that I should just 'get over it'! They have no idea what they're talking about!"

Hillary smiled. "You look adorable in that outfit, by the way."

"Thanks," Macy answered as she looked at herself in the mirror. "But?"

"But I think that maybe they're right." Seeing that Macy was about to protest, Hillary held up her hand to stop her. "Here me out. Let's look at this logically. You are an amazing person and gorgeous to boot, living in a small town with few options for dating. A hot guy recently moved to town, and he's taken an interest in you." She pointed her finger at Macy. "Am I missing something here?"

"Yes!" Macy exclaimed. "You're missing the fact that he's my boss!"

"Oh, please," Hillary dismissed her. "That's the only reason you can come up with?"

Macy looked at her friend for over a year. As tears began to form, she said, "You think you know me so well, but you don't. I'm not as wholesome as you think I am."

Hillary felt compelled to hug Macy. "Look, honey, we've all done things we aren't proud of. But that shouldn't keep you from finding happiness when it's staring you in the face. Everyone in town knows Jake is perfect for you. Why don't you?"

Macy looked at her friend and wiped a tear from her cheek. "It just wouldn't work. I wish I could tell you more, but I'm just not ready."

Hillary smiled at Macy. "Okay. When, and if you need someone, I'm here for you."

"Thanks."

"Alright, let's get you some new clothes," Hillary said, turning Macy around to face the mirror. "I guess that you haven't been shopping in a while."

Macy mouthed "thank you" to her friend as she looked at her from the mirror. Hillary was right. It had been a long time since Macy had gone shopping.

By the time she had finished over an hour later, Macy had purchased all the items she had picked out. But she knew that she had just received more than a new wardrobe in the transaction.

As she left the store, Macy began to wonder if all the excuses she had for not dating Jake were just that, excuses. However, she had spent so much time building a wall to protect herself from being hurt again, and she wasn't sure if she could dismantle it that easily. Sometimes it was just easier to hide behind it than to put herself out there again.

Macy was so deep in thought she didn't hear Chandler yelling her name from across the street. It wasn't until Chandler had crossed and was standing right in front of her that Macy realized she'd had been trying to get her attention. "Oh, sorry," Macy apologized, "guess I have a lot on my mind."

"Clearly," Chandler said, laughing, "I've been yelling your name so loud that everyone in town heard it but you! What's got you so preoccupied?"

"Oh, I was just thinking about all the new clothes I got and wondering where I was going to wear them." Macy chose to go the safe route and not let on that her feelings for Jake might be changing. "Did you want anything in particular?"

"Yes. I'm heading over to pick up lunch for Peter and the guys and wondered if you'd mind helping me carry everything. But I can see you already have your hands full," Chandler explained, pointing to the large bag Macy was holding. "If you don't mind, maybe Andrea would stash it in her back office so your hands would be free to help me."

"Sure, I'd be glad to help!" Macy wanted to see the progress in the park anyway.

"Andrea, can I stash my bag in your office while I help Chandler with her delivery?" Macy asked as they entered the diner.

"Sure thing," Andrea answered, pointing toward the office in the back. "Looks like you hit the jackpot at Hillary's."

"Yes, she did," Chandler answered for Macy. "Now we just need to find a place and reason for her to wear all her new clothes."

"Oh," Andrea smiled, "I'm sure we can arrange something."

Macy scowled at both of her friends. "I don't need you two to 'arrange' anything for me. I can take care of myself just fine."

"Whatever you say, Macy," Andrea answered. "I think your order is just about ready, Chandler. Should I put this on Peter's tab?"

"Yep, I'm not paying for all this food!" Chandler assured her. As she looked into one of the bags, she asked, "All the paper products in here as well?"

One of Andrea's employees assured her that he had packed everything they would need for their box lunches. "We decided just to make the box lunches and made eight of them. If you have any extras, I'm sure the workers will finish it off."

"Definitely," Chandler said as she picked up the handles of one of the bags. "However, I think there were six of them, and with the two extra, that means Macy and I can eat as well. Good thinking!"

"Oh, good. I'm starved!" Macy stated, rubbing her belly. "I probably shouldn't be since I had that cinnamon roll at your place this morning, but shopping takes a lot of energy."

"I know," Chandler agreed. "Thanks again, Andrea. You're the best!"

As Chandler and Macy carried bags containing the box lunches, complete with a sandwich, chips, cookie, and drink, over to the park, Macy saw that one of the workers was Jake. Her first thought was, *how can he look so great, all hot and sweaty?* But her second thought was, *am I ready for this? Guess now is as good a time as any to see if I'm willing to relax and let whatever happens, happen.*

Chapter 16

After Jake finished his run on Saturday, he changed into work clothes and went to see if Peter needed help at the park since he was already sweaty. Maybe it was time for a little male bonding.

"Hey, Jake!" Peter yelled as Jake walked up to the gazebo. "Here to help?"

"Yes, I am," Jake answered. "Tell me what you want me to do, and I'll do it."

"Well, alright. We're getting ready to set these railings and could use some help holding them." Peter told Jake where to hold them so they could be set into place. "All moved in?"

"Yes," Jake said, "and a little restless, so I decided to come to bug you." He wasn't sure what it was, but try as he might, he couldn't concentrate in his new home. Something kept telling him to go to the park.

"Maybe it was Maggie and Horace telling you to get out and meet people," Peter joked.

Jake just looked at him dumbfounded. "Have you been reading my mind?"

"Oh, you can't be serious!?" Peter all but shouted. "I was only kidding!"

"Well, since you brought it up," Jake decided to take the opening, "Do you believe in all these ghost stories?"

"Yeah, I kinda do," Peter answered. "I know it sounds weird, but I did see the couple down by the lake the night I thought I had lost Chandler for good. Something about seeing them together and their love for each other made me want to fight for her even more."

"That's just crazy," Jake commented. "I mean, I hardly think Maggie and Horace are haunting my house."

"Maybe not, but I wouldn't rule it out," Peter said. "Now, let's get these railings set. Chandler's bringing lunch soon."

Peter, Jake, and the rest of the crew completed setting the railings just as Chandler showed up with lunch from the diner. And she wasn't alone. Jake was happy to see that Macy was with her. As he watched her walk over to the picnic tables, Jake realized that this was one of the few times he'd seen Macy not dressed in scrubs.

Looking at her now, he saw she'd dressed in navy shorts and a pink and white tank top that flowed in what slight breeze there was. For as hot as the air temperature was, Macy looked relaxed and comfortable. Her long red hair was pulled back off her face, giving her an even more youthful appearance. *Man, she's beautiful,* he thought.

"Yay, the cavalry is here just in time!" Peter said enthusiastically. "I think the men were about to mutiny." He turned to his crew. "Come on, guys. Let's eat!"

Chandler and Macy passed out box lunches to the four men who were on Peter's payroll first. "God bless you guys for coming out in this heat," Chandler said as she looked around at all that the guys had done since earlier that morning. "You've gotten so much accomplished!"

Peter took a lunch from her and kissed her on the cheek. "And we're on track to be finished by the end of the day. That is if this guy," he continued pointing to Jake, "sticks around and helps. You don't have to go home and clean your house or anything, do you?"

"This guy," Macy said, handing a box to Jake, "has a cleaning lady."

Jake just stared at Macy as he sat down next to her. "I don't have a cleaning lady," he denied.

Macy opened the top of her soda can and took a drink. "But I saw her sweeping your kitchen floor at six-thirty this morning."

"Macy, you can see Jake's kitchen floor from your house?" Peter asked, opening his box and unwrapping his chicken salad sandwich. "Oh, my, this smells heavenly," he gushed as he took a huge bite.

"Enough about your lunch." Chandler gently slapped him on the arm. "Macy, you saw someone sweeping Jake's floor?"

Macy looked back and forth from Chandler to Peter to Jake. "Okay, yes, I can see into Jake's kitchen," she admitted. "But that just means that he can see my front porch, so I'd say we're even."

Chandler waved her hand. "Macy, I couldn't care less if you could see straight through to his shower. I want to get back to the part about his cleaning lady. What did she look like?"

Macy put down her drink. "Well, she was about my height, wearing a dark blue dress, and had her white hair put up in a bun on the top of her head. Honestly, Jake, I have no idea how you could hire an old lady to clean up after you!?" She gave him a very disgusted look.

Jake put down his sandwich. "First of all, I would never be so cold as to hire someone who, from the sounds of it, could be my grandmother. And second, for the last time, I don't have a cleaning lady!"

The table got unusually quiet as all four looked from one to the other. Peter was the first to speak. "Then who was the woman Macy saw?" he asked cautiously.

"Chandler, what did Maggie look like?" Macy asked hesitantly.

Chandler gave a small smile. "Just as you described."

"Oh no!" Jake all but shouted. "My house is not haunted!" By now, the other four men who had been sitting at their table minding their own business began listening more intently.

"You know," one of them said, "my aunt lived in my grandmother's house after she passed. She claimed Grandmother spoke to her all the time."

"I'm a doctor, for heaven's sake! You can't possibly expect me to believe in ghosts! It's just not practical!"

"Well, I guess that means that you did hire a little old lady who comes and cleans your house at six-thirty in the morning, just like Macy said," Peter told him, smiling, as he picked up his cookie. "Are these yours, Chandler?"

Chandler nudged him in the side. She turned to Jake. "Look, it's not that bad, especially if she's sweeping your floors. Isn't that one of the things the construction workers said happened when they were renovating the place?"

Jake rubbed his hand over his face. "Yes. I suppose it could be worse. She could be leaving messes for me to clean up instead of the other way around."

"If I were you, though," Peter said, pointing his finger at Jake, "I probably wouldn't be walking around in my skivvies."

"Why, so I don't shock the ghost of Maggie?" Jake asked sarcastically.

Peter started laughing. "No, you idiot, because Macy can see right into the back of your house!"

Macy turned to Jake and flipped her hands up, giving him the universal 'oh well' sign. "At least I know all you can see is my front porch. No chance of seeing anything there except me drinking my wine." She popped a chip into her mouth and smiled.

"I think I need to go shopping for curtains," Jake said to no one in particular.

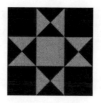

Chapter 17

Chandler and Macy left the men to finish working on the park. As they headed back to the diner for Macy to retrieve the bag she'd left earlier, they passed Myrtle and Mabel sitting on the bench outside the bakery.

"Did you girls have a nice lunch?" Myrtle asked while looking straight ahead toward the street.

Macy thought she detected a note of sarcasm in Myrtle's voice. She and Chandler exchanged glances before she confirmed that, yes, indeed, they had had a nice lunch.

"Glad to know you're still speaking to us," Mabel remarked, somewhat apologetically. Mabel hated for people to be mad at her.

"Mabel, you're so sweet. I could never be mad at *you*," Macy assured her, making it clear she didn't think Mabel was at fault for Myrtle's earlier rudeness at Hillary's.

Mabel smiled at her while Myrtle continued looking straight ahead. Ignoring Macy's comment, Myrtle turned the conversation to the park renovations. "Chandler," Myrtle began, looking in Chandler's direction, "Does Peter still think the park will be ready for the Labor Day celebration? I know the mayor has big plans."

"Yes, Peter said it would be tight, but they'll finish in time. That's why they're working on a Saturday," Chandler explained. "He even enlisted Jake's help."

"Looks like there's still work to do around the playground," Myrtle noted. "The pirate ship structure and all the other new pieces look like lots of fun, but not too safe for children to play on."

"Peter said something about lots of mulch that will need to be spread to make it safe for the kids," Chandler agreed. "Several truckloads of mulch, making it a pretty huge project."

A couple of parents heard Chandler's comment as they walked by and stopped. "You know," one of them told the group, "Coach Franks was just saying at practice today that he'd like to find a community service project for the team to do to show their appreciation to the town for supporting them. I wonder if they could spread the mulch."

"Really?!" Chandler asked excitedly. "That would be great! I'll tell Peter to contact the coach to set it up."

"I'll let the coach know as well," the parent said. As the parents continued down the street, Macy thought she heard one of them say something about the hot new doctor and his nurse. She prayed she was wrong, or at the very least that Myrtle hadn't heard. No such luck.

"So, Dr. Grainger likes his nurse, huh?" Tapping her finger to her wrinkled cheek, Myrtle continued, "Wonder if Mary's husband knows the doctor has the hots for his wife?"

Macy looked at her older friend. "Honestly, Myrtle. Will you just let it drop?" Seeing Myrtle just smile and adjust her floral top, Macy turned to Chandler. "I'm going to get my stuff and go home. I have better things to do than stand here and be part of Myrtle's speculations."

"Before you go, come into the bakery. I have something to show you," Chandler said, linking her arm with Macy and guiding her in the direction of the bakery. "Bye, ladies. Try to stay cool in the heat."

Once they entered the coolness of the bakery, Chandler pointed to a corner table, silently ordering Macy to take a seat. She returned a few minutes later with tall glasses of ice water for each of them. "It's not wine on my front porch, but it'll have to do."

Macy knew Chandler was referring to their counseling/wine drinking sessions they frequently had in the evenings. Many a night, they discussed their concerns and grievances over a bottle of Merlot or Chardonnay.

Macy took a drink of the cool water, letting the icy liquid go down, trying to cool her temper over Myrtle's latest attempt to create a relationship that wasn't there. "I don't know why I let her get to me," Macy said, frustratingly pushing back loose strands of hair that had escaped sometime during the day. "I know they all mean well, but I'd just like to tell them to butt out." She knew deep down that she'd never be able to do that.

Chandler took the time to wipe some of the condensation from her glass before she spoke. She knew where Macy was coming from, having been the Little Old Lady Network's focus not too long ago. But for as much as she hated to admit that Myrtle and her posse were right, if it weren't for their persistence, she may have never given Peter the time of day. "Macy, I know they can be a bit overwhelming," she started before Macy interrupted.

"A bit overwhelming?!" Macy shouted. "Every time I turn around, there they are. I couldn't even enjoy shopping at Hillary's this morning. While I was in the dressing room, I could hear Myrtle and Mabel come in the store talking. And I was the topic of conversation!" She was trying hard not to cry again.

Chandler reached over and placed a sympathetic hand on Macy's. "What were they saying?" She knew Myrtle had a tendency toward speaking before thinking.

Macy looked at her closest friend in the whole world. "That I had to 'get over whatever it is' that has me so against Jake. I talked a little to Hillary after they left and had pretty much convinced myself that maybe I should. Some of my outfits I picked out with Jake in mind, wondering if he would like them." She smiled through unshed tears.

"That's good," Chandler said encouragingly.

"And then I surprised myself by having a really good time at lunch teasing him about Maggie and Horace."

"You did seem much more relaxed," Chandler agreed.

"All was going well until we saw Myrtle and Mabel again." Macy wiped a tear from her cheek. "I wish they would just leave me alone," she moaned. "I'm not as quick to move into a relationship as you were, Chandler," referring to the short amount of time Chandler and Peter had dated before he asked her to marry him. "I don't think Myrtle understands that."

Chandler tried to reassure Macy that Myrtle's intentions were all good and not spiteful. "I'm sure she only has your best interests at heart. Unfortunately, along with her romantic side, she also has an impatient side. Would you like for me to talk to her to see if I can get her to let you take things at your own pace?"

Macy smiled for the first time since lunch. "That would be great. Hopefully, she'll listen to you."

"It's worth a try," Chandler answered, smiling. "And if that doesn't work, we'll have Jake prescribe castor oil again!"

Macy managed a smile. "Thanks for making me laugh."

They talked for a few more minutes about wedding plans before Macy looked at her watch and saw that it was after three o'clock. "I'd better go and let you close. I have some cleaning to do anyway."

"Let's go out to the winery this evening. You can wear one of your new outfits," Chandler suggested, smiling.

"And of course, you'll want to invite Jake as well," Macy replied, knowing full well that was Chandler's intention.

"Do you have a problem with that?" Chandler asked.

"No, just making sure," Macy said with a wink. "Let me know what time to be ready," she told her friend as she hugged her goodbye.

"I'll text you," Chandler said before locking the door behind Macy and flipping the sign to 'closed'. She turned to see that Gretchen and Luann had already done the closing duties and were standing there, purses in hand.

"You guys are the best," Chandler told them. "Luann, we are going to miss you when you go back to college on Wednesday." Chandler knew she'd have high school kids after that, but they couldn't work as many hours as Luann had.

"You have me until Tuesday," Luann assured her. "I'll do the bank drop."

Chandler locked up the bakery and headed back out into the August heat. She walked back over to the park to tell Jake and Peter about her winery plans. Once they confirmed to meet at Chandler's at six-thirty that evening, she texted Macy. Chandler was looking forward to getting Macy out of Hope Springs and away from Myrtle's spies. She hoped then Macy would be able to relax and see where things led with Jake.

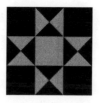

Chapter 18

Macy looked at her reflection in the full-length mirror on the back of her closet door. She chose to wear the blue maxi with yellow flowers that she had picked up at Hillary's. Hillary was right; she did feel beautiful in the dress. With her hair pulled back off her face and secured by a pearl barrette, she let the back fall softly over her shoulders. She applied more make-up than she had in a long time, never really feeling the need to for work.

As she slipped into little strappy sandals, Macy was glad she took the time to paint her toes a soft shade of pink. She found herself realizing that she was looking forward to the evening. And while she still wasn't comfortable with the thought of dating her boss, she knew he wasn't married so that history wouldn't be repeating itself.

Macy looked around at her little house. For the first time in her life, she finally felt settled. Her upbringing was nothing like Chandler's. She didn't have grandparents to take over raising her when her own parents let drugs rule their lives. Macy had gone from foster home to foster home from the age of six, never feeling like she belonged in any of them.

The one thing she did do right was to graduate from high school with honors. Fortunately, once she entered high school, she was only in two foster homes, and they were in the same school district. While Macy wasn't active in extracurricular activities, she did have a great guidance counselor who helped her to achieve her dream of going to nursing school, on a full scholarship, no less.

Upon graduation, she said goodbye to the last foster home, got a job to help pay her minimal rent in a shared apartment close to campus, and worked hard to graduate in three years.

The one thing that was lacking in her life was love. When she graduated from nursing school and began working for her previous employer, she thought she'd found that love. Unfortunately, she'd found out six months later that he was already married. Macy had been crushed. But God works in mysterious ways, and Macy learned the next day about the opening in Hope Springs. She jumped at the chance and moved to town three weeks later. And while she didn't own this home, she still thought of it as hers and took great care in decorating every square inch of it.

Love still eluded her, but maybe with Jake, that could change. Macy decided that Myrtle might be right, but she refused to let the older woman know that, at least until she was sure. She wasn't about to get her hopes up yet, but she was going to be open-minded.

*****

Jake had spent the entire day helping Peter at the park. The work wasn't particularly hard, just grueling in the heat. The highlight of the day was lunch with Chandler and Macy. He had never seen Macy so relaxed. He hoped it continued when they went to the winery.

As he walked into his cottage, Jake was reminded again of their lunch conversation. "Hey, Maggie and Horace, I'm home!" he shouted. After getting no response, he decided Macy must have been seeing things.

123

Jake went to take a shower and get ready. He had less than an hour until they were meeting at Chandler's. Luckily, the humidity had broken sometime during the afternoon, and the temperature was cooling down.

Dressed in khaki pants, a powder blue polo, and loafers, Jake headed out the door forty-five minutes later. As he turned to lock the door, he shouted back into the house, "Bye Maggie and Horace! Have a good evening!" He could have sworn he heard a woman whisper, "You too." *It must have been the wind,* Jake thought.

Jake walked around the block to Chandler's just as Macy came from her house across the street. Even from a distance, Jake could see she'd taken time to fix her hair differently and apply more make-up than what she usually wore. She was beautiful, plain and simple.

*****

Macy picked up her purse and keys off the small table by the front door and stepped out onto the front porch. She noticed that at least the humidity wasn't as oppressive as earlier. After locking the front door behind her, Macy turned to see Jake rounding the corner and heading up the sidewalk. She refused to consider why her stomach did a flip at the sight of him. She thought he looked terrific when he was in his exercise clothes but dressed in khakis and a blue polo; he was devastatingly handsome. Macy once again found that she was looking forward to their evening.

"Hi," Macy said as she walked across the street toward Chandler's.

"Hi, yourself," Jake answered, smiling. "You look beautiful," he added quietly.

Macy tilted her head to look at him. "You clean up pretty good yourself, Dr. Grainger."

Jake waved his finger at her. "Tonight, it's Jake and Macy."

"Ok, Jake," Macy agreed.

"Don't you two look fabulous all cleaned up!" Chandler said excitedly as she and Peter stepped out onto her front porch.

"Yeah," Peter agreed. "Of course, Macy looks good in everything, but Jake, you clean up nice."

"You make it sound like I'm usually a slob," Jake countered. "I'm more dressed up for work than this. I usually have a tie on under my lab coat."

"Yeah, about that," Macy said, touching Jake on the arm. "You could probably lose the tie. I don't remember Dr. Howard ever wearing one."

"Really?" Jake asked, liking the sensation of Macy's hand on his arm probably more than he should have.

"Yep, business casual is just fine in Hope Springs," Macy answered, removing her hand. She noted it still felt warm from touching him.

"Shall we go?" Chandler asked, heading toward her SUV. "We're taking my car since Peter's back seat can barely fit one person, let alone two."

"Oh, I don't know," Peter remarked, hugging his bride-to-be to his side. "I don't recall you ever complaining about it being too small before," he teased.

Chandler playfully slapped him on the arm. "Oh, stop. Nothing like that has ever happened!"

Chandler handed Peter the keys, and they all took their seats and buckled up. As they backed out of the drive, Jake looked through the backyard to the back of his house. Just like Macy said, you could see in his kitchen window. And he could have sworn he saw a little old woman smiling and waving from the same window. He quickly looked to see if any of the others had been looking. When he looked back, she was gone. *I'm going crazy,* he thought.

"What do you think, Jake?" Chandler asked from the front seat.

It was then that Jake realized he had missed part of the conversation. "Think about what?" he asked.

"Where were you just now?" Peter joked, "Chandler wanted to know if we thought the football team would be able to help spread all the mulch."

"Oh, sorry. I think that's a great idea. I know the team has a pretty light practice on Saturday because they work them so hard during two-a-days. And I'm sure if we offered to feed them, then they'd do it. If they're anything like my high school team, they will do anything for food," he finished, laughing.

"You played in high school?" Chandler asked Jake.

"Yep, linebacker, all four years," he answered. "I was fortunate not to have any big injuries, aside from a sprained ankle here or there."

"Did you want to go on to play in college?" Chandler asked.

As Macy sat looking out at the Virginia landscape on the way to the winery, she was thrilled she was finally learning something personal about Jake. But she was a little sad too because she never got to experience football games or anything extra while in school.

"Macy, did you play any sports in high school?" Jake asked. "I know. I bet you were a cheerleader," he answered for her.

"A cheerleader?!" Macy asked, clearly surprised he'd think she'd be a cheerleader. "No, I spent most of my after-school time working to save money for college," she said wistfully. "And besides, if I did have time, I certainly wouldn't have been a cheerleader."

"Why not?" Jake asked, clearly surprised that she would think being a cheerleader was somehow degrading. "I think you would have made a great one."

"Well, I'm not sure what they were like in your school, but in mine, they were the mean girls of the class," Macy answered, thinking back to the many times they had teased her throughout high school. "I would hope that I wasn't like that."

"Definitely not you, Macy," Chandler assured her.

Once they had pulled into the winery parking lot and exited their car, Chandler and Peter lead the way, holding hands. Jake looked down at Macy and cautiously placed his hand in the small of her back, leading them toward the outdoor patio. She looked up at him with a smile that told him it was okay with her.

The hostess seated them at a table overlooking the valley. Macy remembered that this was the same winery they had taken Chandler to a few days before Peter had proposed. She also remembered the sunsets there were spectacular.

Peter chose a bottle of Merlot for the table, and the ladies picked out a couple of appetizers to start. Macy sat back in her chair and took in the scenery. The winery was nestled between two of Virginia's mountain ranges in the Shenandoah Valley region. The patio offered panoramic views of the valley and surrounding mountains.

The main restaurant was housed in a building pre-dating the Civil War. The owners had restored the fifteen-room mansion and turned it into a bed and breakfast as well, making this a wedding destination for many couples. They had erected a beautiful gazebo overlooking the western mountain ridge, offering spectacular sunset views for an evening wedding. Macy wondered what it would be like to get married in such a beautiful place. Knowing that she would have to pay for her own wedding, she sadly knew that would never be an option.

"This is awesome," remarked Jake, looking around in awe. "You would never see anything like this in the city. A man could definitely get used to this view."

"I know," Peter agreed. "And I bet the skiing is great in the winter."

"True," Chandler said, "but usually they have to make snow."

"Really?" asked Jake.

"Yep. We're lucky if we get a really good storm every three years or so," Chandler explained.

After Peter approved the wine he'd chosen, the waitress poured each person a glass. Peter raised his glass in toast. "To good friends, new relationships, and love."

"Beautiful," Chandler said wistfully.

Later, as the two couples walked down by the large fire pit on the property, Jake took a chance and reached for Macy's hand. To his great relief, she didn't slap it away but placed her hand in his. As they followed Peter and Chandler, he enjoyed the feel of her smaller hand.

Macy loved the sensation she got of being cared for by Jake. For the first time in her life, she felt secure and protected.

As they reached the fire pit, they saw that the winery had provided the makings for s'mores. "Oh, I haven't had s'mores since I was in girl scouts!" Chandler said excitedly.

"I've always wanted to try s'mores," Macy said, equally as excited. "We never had anything like this growing up."

Jake was learning by bits and pieces that Macy's upbringing wasn't as traditional as his had been. It made him want to know her story even more. "Well, allow me to teach you to roast the perfect marshmallow," he told her, moving to the table. "The trick is to have the rest of the sandwich ready before you roast the marshmallow." He picked up two graham cracker squares and a chocolate candy bar square and handed them to her. "You hold these while I roast the marshmallow," he said, picking up a roasting stick and marshmallow from the tray.

They walked over to the big fire pit, and Jake squatted down and stuck the marshmallow-covered stick over the red, glowing embers. "Most people just stick the thing in the flame, but to get it just right, it's best to roast it in the embers." He rotated the stick so the marshmallow could turn a golden brown on all sides. Then, just before it caught fire, he pulled it out and brought it over to Macy.

"Now hold out the half with the chocolate on it." Macy did as Jake instructed and watched as he placed the marshmallow-covered stick on the chocolate. "Now take the other graham cracker square and place it on top of the marshmallow and hold it there." As Macy did, Jake carefully pulled the stick out, leaving the marshmallow in the middle of the sandwich.

"Tada!" Jake exclaimed. "Now you get the first bite since you are a s'mores virgin," he said, encouraging Macy to bite into the gooey confection.

As Macy bit into the s'more, she thought she'd died and gone to Heaven. With a groan, she remarked, "This is by far the best thing I've ever eaten. How could I have gone without this for so long?" She continued eating until she had finished the entire sandwich.

Jake smiled and wiped a small amount of marshmallow from her cheek. "I have the feeling there are a lot of experiences you missed growing up," he said quietly. "We'll have to remedy that."

Macy stared into Jake's eyes, not quite sure of how to respond to his comment. She had missed so many things growing up, but he couldn't possibly know to what extent her upbringing was different from his. Somewhere in the background, she could hear laughter and talking, but at that moment, her focus was on the look in Jake's eyes and the feel of his hand on her cheek. The crackle of the fire and sparks flying near finally broke the spell.

"It seems that sparks are flying everywhere tonight," Peter said to Chandler.

"And I couldn't be happier about it," she said, hugging her fiancé.

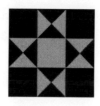

Chapter 19

"We're actually going to finish this quilt tonight," Rosie addressed the ladies of the Advice Quilting Bee. They had all finished their potluck salad dinner and were gathering around the quilt frame. "Myrtle and I have already been working on piecing a Christmas quilt. It is to be auctioned off by the elementary school PTA to raise money for presents for children in need in our community. It still amazes me that we have so many children in Hope Springs who may not have a proper Christmas."

"I know," Fran agreed. "I can't tell you how many times I've had little children come in with their moms to the mercantile wanting this toy or that, but mom has to tell them there is no money that week for extras. It's so sad."

Macy sat working on her stitching and listening to the conversation going on around her. What these lovely women didn't know was that she was one of those children—a product of the foster care system. Sometimes charitable groups such as this one would provide a toy and clothing item, but there wasn't always enough to go around. And the older she got, the less she received. The younger children were taken care of first, which got her to thinking.

"Do we know the ages of the children being helped?" she asked the group.

"Well, no, we don't," Rosie said, thoughtfully. "I would guess all different ages, but that may not be the case. Why do you ask?"

"I just knew of some kids when I was growing up who were in the same boat as these children. I remember them saying that as they got older, the presents seemed to go to the younger children," Macy explained, hopefully not letting on to her own situation. "Everyone wants to help the little ones, but I would just hope that the older children wouldn't be forgotten."

Myrtle put down her needle and took off her glasses. "That's a good point. It's kind of like when we were kids, Rosie. The families with many children often stopped giving presents at a certain age so the little ones could experience the magic of Christmas."

"Very true," Rosie agreed. "I do remember that being the case with some of our larger families."

"It might be a good idea if we could find out from the PTA the different ages and find some way of taking care of the older children as well," Andrea said. "I'd be happy to come up with some sort of fundraiser at the diner. Maybe I could have a dish on the menu where all the proceeds would go to this cause or something like that."

"I could do the same at the bakery," Chandler volunteered. "Older kids' toys are so much more expensive than younger ones these days."

Macy couldn't help but get a little choked up from all the love and support these women showed for children that they probably had never met. "You all are wonderful," she said quietly, fighting to hold back the tears threatening to fall down her cheeks. "Really wonderful."

The others were a little taken aback by the emotional response their gestures had elicited. Rosie got up from her seat and walked over to Macy. She leaned over and gave her a big hug. "We are all family here, in Hope Springs, whether related or not," Rosie assured her. But Rosie knew there was something else Macy wasn't telling. A little more of her past leaked out, and Rosie wasn't sure if anyone else had picked up on it.

Macy wiped her shed tears and picked up her needle. "We'd better stop all this and get to work, or we'll never get Katrina's quilt finished."

Picking up on Macy's desire to change the subject, Chandler announced that the football team would be spreading mulch on the new playground on Saturday. "Peter was so happy the coach wanted the team to do this for the town. He said that was the last big job that would need to be done to make the park renovation complete and ready for the Labor Day celebration."

"Oh, that's wonderful!" Hillary exclaimed. "My kids have been bugging me ever since they saw that pirate ship being installed. I told them it wasn't safe yet because the men hadn't put the mulch down yet. Of course, they argued that a pirate ship is in water, not mulch."

Rosie chuckled at that. "Well, they do have a point there. Aren't children wonderful with how they see things so literally?"

"Unfortunately, they wanted to turn the bathtub into a pirate ship the other night and almost overflowed the water onto the floor so the ship could float!" Hillary shouted.

Myrtle laughed out loud. "Your kids are a handful, aren't they?!"

"Yes, Myrtle, they are. That's why we need to open the playground, and I'm looking forward to them starting back to school as well. Between the two, they'll be too tired for anything else," Hillary laughed.

"So back to the football team," Andrea began, redirecting the conversation. "Who will be feeding them? Because those boys don't do anything unless there is the promise of food."

"Oh, we're off the hook on that one," Chandler answered. "The coach said that since they were performing community service, the boosters would be taking care of it. I think they also wanted a trial run on the new concession stand they recently finished. They now can cook hot dogs and hamburgers, so I'm guessing that's what they'll do."

"Good idea," Andrea agreed.

The ladies continued stitching in silence a bit longer, each working on the design Mary Ann had carefully drawn. "Ladies, we're getting good at this," Mary Ann said, looking around at everyone's work. "This just shows what a great teacher Rosie is. You all are very uniform in your stitches."

They all smiled very proudly. "It's taken a lot of practice and patience, but it looks lovely," Rosie agreed.

The group had talked about so many different topics during the evening that Macy thought she might be off the hook. No one had even mentioned Jake's name.

"So, Macy," Myrtle asked as if reading her thoughts, "how are things going at the medical center?"

"Very busy with school starting next week," Macy answered, continuing her stitching. She knew what Myrtle was getting at and wasn't going to show annoyance.

Chandler looked at Macy and grinned. "Candy, we miss Luann at the bakery. And she's only been gone one day!"

"I know. I miss her at home, too," Candy answered quietly. "She loved working at the bakery, and you and Gretchen taught her so much."

"She's a hard worker. She'll do great when she opens her bed and breakfast," Chandler said encouragingly.

"Yeah, yeah, we all miss Luann," Myrtle said about her granddaughter. "But Macy, what we really want to know is how things are going with you and Jake?"

"Myrtle, I don't think that's our business," Rosie admonished. "Macy, you don't have to tell us if you don't want to."

"Thank you, Rosie," Macy said, grateful to Rosie for setting Myrtle straight. "Myrtle, my relationship, or lack thereof, with Jake really shouldn't be taking up so much of your time. I think your time would be better spent focusing on more productive things like our Christmas project for the children." Macy picked up her needle and continued stitching, sending a signal to Myrtle that this topic was closed.

"Well said," Fran agreed, and upon seeing the shocked expression on her friend's face, replied, "Myrtle, I think Macy is right. Let's let the young people live their own lives without our interference for once. We all love you and know you always have the best of intentions, but if Macy doesn't want our help, then we should respect her wishes."

Myrtle looked around the quilting frame at the women who meant more to her than anyone else in the world. They were all looking at her expectantly. "And you all agree?" she asked the group. Upon seeing everyone shake their heads in the affirmative, Myrtle got up and walked over to Macy. Placing her hand on Macy's shoulder, she said, "I promise not to interfere in your relationship, or lack thereof, with Jake. Although, I don't think the 'or lack thereof' is necessary since we all know something is going on," she said, using air quotes. "However, if you ever feel the need to talk about anything or need our help in moving things along in any way, please know that we're all here for you."

Macy rose from her chair and hugged Myrtle. "Thank you," she said, fighting back the tears she hadn't known were coming. "You all mean the world to me, and if I need anything, I know that I can always come to you. I just don't want to be the topic of conversation all around town."

"It may be too late for that," Andrea remarked. "You and Jake are more popular than politics in the diner, for which I, for one, am eternally grateful. Much less argumentative."

"Ugh, really?" Macy asked, flopping back down in her chair.

"Afraid so," Fran agreed. "Same thing in the mercantile."

"Well, now that we've established that the topic of Macy and Jake has overtaken politics in our little town, how about if we get back to finishing this quilt tonight," Rosie said, looking around the frame to see how much was left to do. "It looks like we don't have much left, so if we all stop talking and start stitching, I think we can finish in the next hour."

Myrtle went back to her seat, and they all got to work. The tradition in the group was the Myrtle and Rosie would place the final stitches in each quilt since they had been the ones to piece the quilt top. And in no time at all, it was time for them to do just that.

"There, another quilt finished by the Advice Quilting Bee," Rosie proclaimed. After a round of applause, Rosie thanked everyone for their hard work. "When you finally stop talking and start stitching, you do stunning work. Now I think it's time for us all to go home and get a good night's sleep. From the sounds of it, our Labor Day weekend is going to be packed full of festivities."

Chapter 20

The Saturday before Labor Day, Hope Springs was alive with activity. Three truckloads of mulch had arrived on Friday, and the football team was hard at work spreading it around the newly finished playground. Peter had also ordered enough to beautify the gardens around the park and the planter boxes lining Main Street. The Hope Springs Garden Club took charge of that project, with the help of high schoolers with wheelbarrows transporting the mulch to the desired location. Pretty much if you had the day off from your regular job, you were working on the revitalization project in one form or another.

Since the medical center was closed on Saturday, that meant Jake and the staff were helping. Suzie and Mary were members of the garden club, so they already had their assignments. There was still painting to be done on the gazebo, so Jake and Macy were working there. Macy looked around at the beehive of activity and realized this was what it was like in a real community. This was something she had never experienced growing up.

Jake must have sensed this because he remarked, "Another new experience for you, huh."

Macy looked at him quizzically. "Are you a mind reader?"

Jake just smiled. "No, just reading the expression of wonder on your face." He went back to painting without saying another word.

Macy continued with her painting job but wondered how it was that Jake could read her so well. It was a little unnerving, for sure. She also thought about all she had missed growing up; just the events of the last week had proven that.

The night before, Jake had asked her to go with him to the football scrimmage. He'd said he wanted to make sure there was a medical staff on-site, but she knew he wanted her to experience a Friday night football game. Even though it was just a scrimmage, it was still something she hadn't done before. They'd had a blast.

After the game, he'd walked her home, and they sat on her front porch step just enjoying the quiet after the noise of the game. When she finally stifled a yawn, they said goodnight. Jake surprised her with a gentle kiss on the cheek before heading home.

Before Macy knew it, she heard Peter asking everyone to gather around. "Thank you all for your hard work today!" he yelled, expressing his gratitude to the masses. "We are ready for the dedication on Labor Day morning at eleven o'clock, with a potluck picnic to follow. See you then!"

Since it was now dinnertime, Peter suggested he, Macy, Jake, and Chandler get some dinner. After dinner at the diner and a few bottles of wine at Chandler's, Macy finally fell into bed a little before midnight. She did, however, remember to set her alarm for church the following day.

Sunday morning, Macy and Chandler took their usual seats with the ladies. The pastor's sermon was about new beginnings, with the end of summer and the start of the fall season. Macy felt it spoke to her and her relationship with Jake. She had spent enough time punishing herself for past transgressions, and it was finally time to forgive herself and move forward.

Once the service was over, Rosie pulled Macy aside. "Would you mind walking me home, dear?" she asked.

"Of course," Macy said excitedly. "You don't mind, do you, Chandler?"

"Absolutely not," Chandler answered, knowing full well this was Rosie's way of having that private conversation with Macy about Jake, just as she'd had about Peter.

Once Rosie and Macy were situated on Rosie's beautiful front porch with sweet tea and cookies, Rosie began. "Macy, now you know we all love you very much and only want what's best for you, but something tells me you are keeping parts of yourself hidden from the view of the group."

Rosie was nothing, if not direct. Macy appreciated that. "Yes, that's true. I guess it's from my upbringing. I was never one to share too much of myself with others for fear of getting hurt in the process."

"I can respect that," Rosie said, taking a sip of her tea. "But just know that if you ever need to talk to anyone, we are all here for you. Even Myrtle," she said, smiling.

Macy took a sip of her tea before continuing. "I've never told anyone what I'm about to tell you, Rosie. Not even Chandler knows everything. But I'm so confused about it all that maybe if you know everything, you can help me sort it all out."

"And please know that it goes no further than this porch unless you want it to," Rosie assured her.

Macy took a deep breath. "Let's just say my parents would have never won any parent of the year awards. I learned very early in life that the only person I could count on was myself. Once I graduated from high school, I was really on my own. I missed out on a lot, but I'm pretty proud of how far I've come."

"But?" Rosie encouraged.

"But I'm not proud of my past love life," Macy said sadly. She was so worried Rosie would think less of her when she found out what she had done, and Macy valued her opinion. "I had an affair with my previous employer." She stopped to see Rosie's reaction. When Rosie said nothing, Macy continued, almost defensively, "When we started dating, I had just begun working at his practice. I had no idea he was married."

Rosie took a long drink of her tea before responding. "Macy, my dear, we have all done things in our lives we aren't proud of. The trick is to learn from these actions and not repeat them. I take it this is a big reason as to why you've been avoiding a relationship with Jake because the situation is similar?"

"Yes," Macy confirmed, rubbing her face with her hands, frustrated with herself. "I know Jake isn't married, but I still can't get past what I've done."

"Well, you were wise to take things one day at a time, and I appreciate your trusting in me to tell me this," Rosie commented. Macy was happy she didn't detect any disapproval in Rosie's tone. "Okay," Rosie continued, "this was how you felt when Jake first came to Hope Springs. How do you feel now?"

"That's the confusing part," Macy told her. "I'm finding myself more and more attracted to him. I'm just afraid of what could happen if it didn't work out. Hope Springs is my home now, and I couldn't possibly think of leaving." Macy had lived there longer than any place in her entire life, but Rosie didn't know all that.

"Why would you need to leave?" Rosie asked, trying to understand where Macy was coming from.

"It's not like there are other places in Hope Springs for a nurse to work," Macy explained. "Jake, as the town doctor, is more important to the community than I am."

"Now, Macy Greenburg!" Rosie rarely raised her voice, but she wanted Macy to hear this, "You are both important for different reasons. Running away wouldn't solve anything. And besides, there isn't any reason to run. As my mother used to say, don't go borrowing trouble. How about if you see what happens before you start planning your escape?"

Macy thought about that for a minute. "So, what you're trying to get through my thick head is I'll never know how it's going to go until I give it a try?"

"Yes, that's a good way of looking at it," Rosie agreed. "Let me ask you this. Do you want to have a relationship with Jake?"

Macy smiled a genuine smile, "Yes, I do."

"Then I don't see the problem. We only have so much time on this earth, so grab the happy times while you can," Rosie advised. "If the bad is going to happen, there's nothing you can do to stop it. Look at all that has happened to get you and Jake to this small town at the same time. I'd

143

say there's a higher power at work here, and as much as she'd like to take credit for it, it's not Myrtle!"

Rosie's right, Macy thought. She spent so much time punishing herself for the past that she was in jeopardy of missing her future. "Thank you," Macy told Rosie through tears threatening to fall. She seemed to be doing a lot of that lately.

"Just an observation, but the few times I've seen you and Jake together, I'd say the feeling's mutual," Rosie said with a knowing smile.

"Well, hello, ladies!" Myrtle yelled from her house across the street.

Rosie stood and turned to Macy. "I think we're done here. You go on, and I'll run interference with Myrtle, so she doesn't give you the third degree."

"Thank you so much for everything," Macy said, hugging her dear sweet friend.

Macy started down the sidewalk as Myrtle was crossing the street. "Where are you going in such a hurry?" Myrtle asked.

Before Macy could respond, Rosie yelled from the porch, "Come on up out of the sun, Myrtle! Macy has other things to do today."

A dejected Myrtle walked up onto the porch. "You know, Rosie, you did the same thing that Sunday you had Chandler here after church. You rushed her off so I couldn't talk to her about Peter."

"I'm doing nothing of the kind," Rosie disagreed. "Macy and I were just having a lovely conversation about the town and its residents."

"Okay, fine. If you aren't going to give me the details of the conversation, then I'm just going to have to draw my own conclusions," Myrtle said, clearly annoyed with her friend. "I'm going to conclude that Macy finally took my advice about Jake," she said smugly.

"Oh, Myrtle." Rosie smiled, handing her friend a cookie.

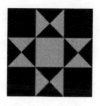

Chapter 21

The Labor Day weather couldn't have been better. The temperature was going to be in the low eighties with very comfortable humidity. As Jake walked into the park a little before noon, he heard someone yelling his name and saw one of his senior patients coming toward him. "Hello, Gertrude," he greeted her, noting she was practically pulling a younger woman with her.

"Hi, Dr. Grainger," Gertrude replied, almost out of breath. "I'd like you to meet my granddaughter, Millie. She's visiting from West Virginia," she finished, practically pushing the girl into Jake.

"Hello, Millie. Welcome to Hope Springs," Jake said, noting the poor girl looked like she wanted to be anywhere else than standing in front of him. Clearly, Gertrude had something on her mind. "How long will you be staying in Hope Springs?"

"That depends," Gertrude answered before Millie could even open her mouth. "I thought you might be available to show her around town." Poor Millie turned beet red and scowled at her grandmother.

"Well," Jake began, trying desperately to figure a way out of this sticky situation. Luckily, Myrtle had been within earshot of the entire conversation and stepped in to help.

"Millie, dear, is that pie for the dessert table?" Myrtle asked, pointing to the pie Jake just noticed Millie had been holding.

"Yes," Millie answered shyly.

"Dr. Grainger, Millie makes the best apple pie in all of West Virginia. She wanted to make sure you got the first piece," Gertrude gushed, continuing to push her granddaughter on Jake.

But Myrtle would have nothing of it. "Okay, Millie, let's get your pie to the dessert table and see if we can find a place for you and your grandmother to sit." As she began ushering the pair toward the food tables, she turned back and winked at Jake.

He mouthed a silent "thank you" and smiled. As he turned to head to where he had seen Peter and Chandler earlier, he heard another of his patients shouting at him from across the lawn. This time it was old Mrs. Miller and someone who looked to still be in high school. He chose to ignore the pair and practically ran to Chandler and Peter. "You have to hide me," he begged them.

"Why?" Peter asked, laughing.

"Apparently, the older residents of this town are using today to introduce their granddaughters to me!" he practically shouted. "If it weren't for Myrtle, I'd be giving Millie a tour of the town right now!"

"Who's Millie?" Peter asked, looking around at the crowd gathering in the park.

"That one," he said, pointing toward the younger woman near the food tables, "the one in the blue dress with glasses."

147

Peter started laughing. "She looks like she just walked off the set of a late eighteen-hundreds movie!"

"Close," Jake said, "she's visiting from West Virginia. I'm sure it's a lovely place, but my guess is she doesn't live in one of the more metropolitan areas."

"You're right," Chandler agreed. "She lives in one of the small towns at the foothills of the Appalachians. She comes to visit Gertrude once a year, and from what I've been told, she thinks Hope Springs is a metropolitan area."

"Oh, Lord," Jake moaned.

"Oh, there you are, Dr. Grainger!" Mrs. Miller shouted. The fact that she was practically in front of Jake when she shouted was not lost on him. "I wanted to introduce you to my granddaughter, Laura. She's visiting from Baltimore, Maryland." Laura, like Millie, looked like she'd rather be anywhere but at a picnic in Hope Springs. But where Millie was shy and seemed a bit overwhelmed, Laura looked bored and downright underwhelmed by the whole thing.

"Hey," Laura greeted him, chomping on her gum.

"Hello, Laura," Jake answered, smiling politely. "How wonderful it is that you get to spend this time with your grandmother."

"Yeah, I guess," she said, clearly not seeing how 'wonderful' the experience was.

"I was hoping you'd be able to show her around town, Dr. Grainger," Mrs. Miller explained. "I know you're new to the town and all, but I figured you'd have some free time for her."

Once again, as Jake was formulating his response, Myrtle came to the rescue. "Now, Lucy, I don't think Dr. Grainger has time in his busy schedule to give Laura a tour of our town. I think it might be better if she drove around, and you could explain the sites to her."

"No, Myrtle, I think it would be much better if Dr. Grainger took her," Mrs. Miller said forcefully.

"Mrs. Miller, are those dishes for the potluck?" Chandler asked, noticing both women holding containers of food.

"Yeah, they are," Laura answered, annoyed. "And this is getting heavy. Where are we supposed to put them, anyway?"

"Follow me, ladies," Myrtle ordered, turning to take the pair to the food tables.

Jake turned and noticed Chandler on her phone texting someone. "Where is Macy, anyway?" he asked, worried he was going to be married off before she got there.

"That's who I'm texting," Chandler said, laughing. "She's on her way now."

"Jake, I'm doing my best, but why do you have to be so darn cute?!" Myrtle exclaimed as she walked back from escorting Mrs. Miller and Laura to the food table. "You'd think this was some kind of matchmaking picnic from the eighteen-hundreds, and all the young ladies were being paraded in front of the eligible bachelor by their grandmothers! So far, have you seen any you like?" she asked, laughing.

Jake looked up to see Macy walking up the sidewalk at the entrance to the park. She was dressed in a cute red, white, and blue sundress with matching sandals. She'd pulled her hair back in a loose ponytail, secured with a red, white, and blue ribbon. She looked gorgeous. It was all Jake could do not to run to her and scoop her up in his arms.

Myrtle looked in Macy's direction. "I'll take that as a 'yes'," she said, smiling. "Chandler, if you hear of any more grandmothers pushing their eligible granddaughters on our young doctor, will you let me know? I'm kind of enjoying being Jake's bodyguard." Of course, who had ever heard of a bodyguard dressed in red spandex pants and a top that looked like the American flag, Jake wondered. The red, white, and blue sneakers and matching headband put the outfit over the top.

"Bodyguard?" Macy asked as she came upon the group. "Why does Jake need a bodyguard? Is he not safe?" She couldn't imagine anyone wanting to harm Jake any more than she could imagine Myrtle being the one in charge of keeping him safe!

"I'll let Jake explain. Is that for the food table?" Myrtle inquired, pointing to the platter of cookies Macy was holding.

"Wait!" Jake held up his hand. "As the town doctor, I need to taste these to make sure they're safe for consumption." He reached for one of the snickerdoodles on the platter.

Peter started laughing. "How come you didn't have to taste the food Millie and Laura were holding?"

Jake just stuck his tongue out at Peter in response and then took a bite of the cookie. "Perfect!" he declared. "Just like the woman who baked them."

150

"I may just throw up," Peter joked, putting his finger in his mouth in a gagging motion.

"Hey, I think that was romantic," Chandler remarked. "How come you never say anything like that about my cookies?" she asked Peter. "Is the romance dead even before the wedding?"

Peter put his arm around Chandler and pulled her close. "Absolutely not; it's just beginning."

"Okay, before you two couples need to get rooms, I'm going to take these to the food table. It's almost noon, and the mayor will be starting the festivities," Myrtle explained before walking off with Macy's platter of snickerdoodles.

Macy wasn't sure what she'd walked into, but she'd gotten Chandler's text telling her she'd better get up there or risk losing Jake. After leaving Rosie's the previous afternoon, Macy had gone home determined to be all in on her relationship with Jake. She'd spent the evening baking the cookies, of course hoping he'd like them, and picking out just the right outfit, again with him in mind.

As she got ready for the day, she thought about her conversation with Rosie. She couldn't change the past, but she could definitely enjoy living in the present and was looking forward to the future. She realized that her relationship with Jake was nothing like her previous romantic debacle, and she couldn't wait to see what each day brought. Then, when she received Chandler's text, she got worried that she'd already blown it.

"So, who is it that's so dangerous you need Myrtle's protection?" Macy asked, looking around at the crowd.

Peter started snickering, Chandler hit him on the arm, and Jake wanted to punch him as well. "You have no competition, Macy. Believe me," Peter said, through his snickers.

Chandler, the voice of reason, apparently, pointed to Millie first, and then Laura. "See, no contest."

"Hmm," Macy looked at both girls and then back at Jake. "So, they are interested in you?"

"Let's just say their grandmothers think I would be a good catch," he answered proudly.

"Well, if that's what you want..." Macy smiled, letting the statement hang in the air.

"No way!" Jake wanted to make sure Macy knew nothing could be further from the truth. And he thought it was time that the rest of the town knew he was not on the market. He knew it was a little impulsive, and he hoped Macy didn't mind, but he took her in his arms and kissed her right there in front of the whole town. Just a quick kiss, but one meant to show that he was taken.

Macy wasn't sure what had just happened. So far, Jake had only kissed her on the cheek. This was so much more, and not just because it was on the lips, but because it was in front of the whole town. He didn't release her hand either as they walked over to where the crowd gathered near the gazebo. She glanced at Rosie, who was sitting a short distance away near the mayor. Rosie gave her an approving smile and an out-of-character thumbs-up sign. Macy smiled back. She was Jake's girl, and she didn't care if it sounded old-fashioned or sexist. Macy was Jake's girl, and she couldn't be happier.

The rest of the day was spent dedicating various parts of the newly renovated park, presenting the mayor with the wall hanging the Advice Quilting Bee had done of Peter's vision for the town, and eating lots and lots of food. Fortunately, there were also games to be played and a local country band to dance to.

As night fell on the festivities, the park lights were turned on so the party could continue. The band played a mix of fast and slow songs, and it was during one of the slow songs that Jake knew he was falling for Macy in a big way. As he held her and they swayed to the music, he looked down into her beautiful blue eyes looking back at him and he knew.

Macy was enjoying the evening so much that she didn't want it to end. As she and Jake danced to a beautiful slow song, she looked up into his eyes and knew she was in love. She wasn't sure when it happened. Maybe it was between eating all the food and watching him play freeze tag with the little kids, but sometime during the day, it happened. And the best part was that she wasn't afraid of the future. She was truly happy for the first time in her life.

As the song ended, Jake bent down and gave Macy a long, slow kiss meant to show her how he felt. He wanted to make sure the whole town knew that his heart was taken.

Off to the side, the Little Old Lady Network sat smiling. "Ladies, I think our town doctor and nurse are off the market," Myrtle stated, smiling.

Rosie also saw what was happening on the dance floor. She was so happy for both of them and prayed for smooth sailing. Unfortunately, she had a feeling Macy was still holding something back. She just hoped it wasn't big enough to ruin their relationship.

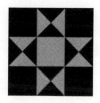

Chapter 22

Thursday afternoon, Macy was busy cleaning up the exam room and restocking supplies. Since it was finally quiet, she had time to reflect on the past few days. After Jake showed everyone, in no uncertain terms, that he and Macy were dating, it seemed that every patient who came in had some kind of comment. Most were positive, but when Mrs. Miller came in for her blood pressure check, it was a little high. Even though she had gained a few pounds since her last appointment, she claimed that it was because Macy had stolen Dr. Grainger away from her granddaughter, Laura. Never mind the fact that Laura was still in high school, making such a relationship illegal.

And when Gertrude came in for a supposed sinus infection, she gave Macy the cold shoulder, requesting that Mary be her nurse from now on instead.

"But Gertrude, Macy has been your nurse since she's been here," Mary explained. "It would be best if she continued with your care."

"No, I don't want her anymore. I want you," Gertrude said defiantly, crossing her arms over her chest and sticking her nose in the air like a two-year-old.

"May I ask why? We need to note it in your record that you have requested a change," Mary said, knowing full well what the answer was going to be.

"Because she stole Dr. Grainger from my Millie, that's why!" Gertrude shouted for the whole office to hear.

"I see," Mary replied, trying not to smile. "Well, alright then. Macy, is it okay with you if I treat Gertrude from now on?"

"Absolutely," Macy said, sweeter than she felt. "We want all our patients to be happy with their care here at the Hope Springs Medical Center."

Other than those two instances, everyone else was pretty positive. She wouldn't have put it past Myrtle to threaten most of the town if they said anything negative.

As Macy was finishing restocking supplies in the exam room, Jake came up behind her. "I guess I'm on my own for dinner tonight?"

Macy was startled by his closeness. "Oh! Yes, we have the Advice Quilting Bee tonight, so I'll be eating there. I'd ask you to join us, but I don't recall a man ever crashing one of our dinners. And besides, I'm protecting you from Myrtle and her posse," she finished, smiling sweetly. She was prepared for the onslaught of questions sure to come about everything that happened at the Labor Day celebration.

"Do you think it'll be that bad?" Jake asked, having no idea what went on at those meetings. "I mean, Myrtle had been pushing for us to get together almost from the start, so she should be happy."

"Oh, she's happy, alright," Macy acknowledged. "Now she's going to want to know each and every detail of each and every date we ever go on."

"Every detail?" Jake asked with a sly grin.

155

"Trust me. I'm not telling her anything more than we've gone out and had a lovely time. That alone will drive her nuts for weeks."

"Well, I think I'll leave all that fun to you." Jake wanted nothing to do with Myrtle and her network. "I'm going to see if Peter wants to meet me at the diner. I sure wish there was a sports bar close by where we could catch Thursday night football over a pitcher of beer and some wings."

"That is the one thing Hope Springs doesn't have," Macy agreed. "Chandler was going to ask Myrtle if she knew why we don't have one. I'll see what I can find out and let you know."

"In the meantime, I guess I'll just have to settle for beer in front of my television," Jake conceded. "If you see my lights on, stop by when you're done."

Macy smiled. "As tempting as that sounds, I may pass. Remember, Mabel is your next-door neighbor and one of Myrtle's spies."

"Oh, the hazards of living in a small town," Jake lamented. "Okay, then I'll see you in the morning." He bent down to give Macy a kiss meant to last until they saw each other again.

"You're pretty lethal, you know that?" Macy said dreamily after he ended the kiss. "I think I'd better get back to work, or I'll be late for dinner."

Jake smiled one of his devastating smiles. "Thanks. I'm glad to know I have that effect on you."

*****

Jake walked out and back to his office to finish some patient charts. While his practice in Hope Springs wasn't nearly as busy as his residency in the city, there was still a lot of paperwork. He finally finished about an hour later, with his stomach growling. He looked at his watch and saw that it was just before six o'clock. He texted Peter and asked to meet him at the diner for dinner. Since Peter was in the same boat with Chandler going to the meeting as well, he knew that if he were in town, Peter would be available.

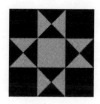

Chapter 22

"So, I guess Dr. Grainger is definitely off the market," Fran commented as the ladies of the Advice Quilting Bee sat working on the Christmas quilt Mary Ann had loaded onto the frame earlier in the day.

"Well, if there was any doubt, Monday night's fireworks took care of that," Myrtle chuckled as she sat threading her needle. "And I'm not talking about those in the sky," she directed at Macy.

Macy had already finished about six inches of the swirl design in front of her and felt pretty proud of how quickly and neatly she was working. "I'm not one to kiss and tell," she said, smiling.

Andrea had also been diligently working on her section of swirls in front of her. "Jake and Peter were having dinner at the diner earlier," she stopped stitching to announce to the group. She couldn't stitch and talk at the same time. "They mentioned something about going back to Jake's to watch the football game, but what they wanted was to go to a sports bar. They were wondering why Hope Springs doesn't have a local watering hole."

Chandler dropped her needle and snapped her fingers. "Oh yeah! I was supposed to ask you all about that. Why don't we have one? I remember grandmother telling stories of you, Myrtle, working in one back in the day."

"Oh, I remember that," Fran told them, taking off her reading glasses and reminiscing. "Myrtle was quite the barmaid back then. And she could entertain on the piano as well."

"Yes, I remember George and I sitting and listening to you play for hours, Myrtle," Rosie added. "Why don't you play anymore?"

Myrtle held up her hands for all to see. "These fingers won't straighten out like they used to. Can't play with crooked fingers," she said gruffly.

"Okay, back this conversation up," Macy said, holding up her hand. "Myrtle, you were a barmaid?!"

"Why does that surprise you, Macy?" Myrtle asked, somewhat defensively.

"Don't get me wrong; I think it's an honorable profession," Macy defended her question. "It's just that I've never seen you drink anything stronger than coffee, even when we have parties at the Hilltop."

Myrtle gave a long, slow smile. "Just because I don't drink it, doesn't mean I don't know how to serve it."

"That's true," Fran agreed. "Myrtle could pour a beer from a tap with just the right amount of foam on top, just as good as any male bartender. In fact, she used to get into trouble with the owner for doing that because she was giving more beer to the customers."

"I don't understand," Macy remarked with a questioning look.

"Well, child," Myrtle began, "if you fill the glass without tilting it, then you get a big head of foam, thus giving the customer less beer. But when I filled the glass, I always tilted it, producing about an inch of foam, making it harder for the beer to spill. I used to argue with Fred, the owner, that it was better for business. I sold way more than the male bartenders," she finished proudly.

"How interesting," Macy said curiously. "But what happened to the bar?"

"When the mill closed, Fred's Place was one of the casualties," Myrtle explained. "I had stopped working there long before, but that's what happened."

"So, it wasn't like some city ordinance or anything?" Chandler asked.

"No," Rosie answered, "just the economy. But now that things are picking up again, maybe it's time for a new establishment to open."

"Anyone interested in opening a bar?" asked Hillary jokingly.

"If the diner weren't such a family establishment, I'd consider getting my liquor license," Andrea said. "I'd be fine with someone opening a new place, as long it was a sports bar or something like that. The Hilltop is our upscale restaurant, and the diner is our everyday family place. We need something a little different."

"It would be nice if it could be downtown, but we don't have any available storefronts right now," Fran agreed. "Of course, that is a great problem to have!"

"I wonder if Peter could incorporate that in one of the buildings he's got going up?" asked Hillary. "It would be

160

nice to have a place to go just for a drink and maybe appetizers. As much as I like the winery, if we had somewhere that we didn't have to drive to, that would be better."

"I'll talk to Peter about it and see if he has any ideas," Chandler told the group.

Everyone settled back into working for a bit longer until Myrtle decided it was too quiet. "So, Macy, do you and Jake have plans for the weekend?"

Macy smiled. She knew Myrtle would come back to the topic again before the night was through. "Well," she put down her needle, "tomorrow night he's taking me out on a fabulous date with dinner, dancing, and entertainment."

Most everyone in the room knew what Friday night in the fall meant, but Myrtle must have had a mental lapse, "Really?!" she asked excitedly. "Do you have details?"

"Yes," Macy began. "While we dine on a three-course dinner, we'll get to watch a show that is so unique, and it's never the same twice."

Myrtle couldn't possibly figure out where Jake would be taking Macy, where the show was never the same twice. "Where is that?"

Looking around and seeing the others, including Rosie, trying to stifle a giggle, Macy announced quite proudly, "the Hope Springs High School football game!" Which brought an eruption of laughter from everyone—but one.

"What?!" Myrtle shouted. "He's taking you to a football game?!"

"Yep, and I'm so excited!" Macy cried.

161

"That was not nice," Myrtle replied, pouting.

"No, that's what you get for being nosy," Rosie admonished.

Macy knew that Myrtle would always be nosy, but for that night, at least, she had put her in her place.

"I love Friday nights in the fall," Hillary said with a sigh. "We get the kids all bundled up if it's cold and head to the stadium. There's nothing like a high school football game to bring the community together."

"Oh, I know what you mean," Rosie agreed. "I remember so many fun times spent with all our friends watching the boys play. The halftime show was my favorite part, though. I just loved watching the kids march."

"The band director was in for dinner last night and said they have over a hundred kids in the marching band this year. Should be quite a show," Andrea told Rosie. "You should come with us tomorrow night."

Rosie thought about that. "You know, I just might do that. It's supposed to be a beautiful evening."

"Peter and I are going and could pick you up if you don't want to walk," Chandler volunteered. "And if you do, we could all walk together."

"Thank you, Chandler. I might just take you up on it," Rosie said. "I'll let you know tomorrow."

"Oh, how fun!" Macy said excitedly. "We can all sit together!"

"You don't mind us crashing your date?" Myrtle asked sarcastically.

"Not at all," Macy told her. She knew that they'd be in a stadium full of people anyway. She was looking forward to experiencing another aspect of small-town life.

Chapter 24

Jake showed up at Macy's promptly at five-thirty the following evening. During work, he had told her that they should be at the field when the teams were warming up if they were needed, though he sure hoped not. There was nothing worse than getting injured before the game even started!

Macy had told him about the events of the previous evening, and he thought she'd handled Myrtle excellently. He'd seen her in action with the older woman in the office, and she knew how to respond in a way that brought Myrtle back to earth.

The more time Jake spent with Macy, the more he realized he'd made the right decision in moving to Hope Springs. He knew the other doctors graduating with him thought he was crazy to give up a lucrative job in the city to become a small-town doctor, but in the short time he'd been in Hope Springs, he'd already come to love it. Even with the Little Old Lady Network and all their quirks, they were still a hoot. To watch them walk around town, usually three or four of them in a little pack with their pocketbooks hanging from their bent arms—it was a riot!

And Myrtle was the best one of all. Her bright dyed-red hair, all curly on top of her head, was usually in sharp contrast to whatever brightly colored top and pants she wore. She reminded him of his own grandmother, with the dangly earrings and costume jewelry she wore around her neck. But Jake knew that deep down, her nosiness was just her way of helping. She had definitely done that at the Labor Day celebration when she'd run interference with Gertrude and Mrs. Miller. He wasn't sure how he would have handled the situation if she hadn't been there.

When Myrtle had come to visit him about his relationship with Macy and informed him about Maggie and Horace, he had thought maybe she'd dyed her hair one too many times. That was until Macy mentioned seeing Maggie in his kitchen window, and then he thought he'd seen her as well. *Maybe it was just my imagination,* he thought, as he stood on Macy's front porch waiting for her to answer the door. He looked over past Chandler's to the back of his house. This time he thought he saw both Maggie and Horace arm in arm at the back window waving at him and smiling. "I'm really losing it," he said out loud as the door opened.

"Losing what?" Macy asked, looking past Jake.

Jake shook his head, trying to clear his brain. He looked back at his house, and of course, there was nothing there. "Nothing," he answered, somewhat unsure of what just happened.

"Did you see Maggie?" Macy asked, somewhat teasingly.

"Okay, I'm sure you think this is funny, but now I saw both Maggie and Horace!" Jake frustratingly rubbed his fingers through his hair. "Should I be worried?"

"Hmmm, I don't know." Macy tapped her finger to her cheek. "Have they done any damage or harmed you in any way?"

Jake could tell she wasn't taking this seriously. "You think all this is funny, don't you?" He didn't think it was funny at all. After all, he was the town doctor and if it got out that he saw ghosts, he thought it could ruin his creditability with his patients. "Do you know what would happen if everyone in town knew I thought I saw ghosts? No one would want to go to a doctor who's crazy!"

Macy could see he was getting worked up over this. She put her hand on his arm and stood on her tip toes to kiss him on the cheek. "Look, no one thinks you're crazy. Everyone in town knows that Maggie and Horace are still there. Personally, I'm not sure I could stay in that house knowing that," she admitted. "You're very brave," she said, smiling.

"Very funny," he said dryly. Jake took a moment to calm his nerves and look at his date for the evening. Macy had chosen to wear a pair of navy capris, tennis shoes, and a red top with white dots. The school colors, he noticed. She'd pulled her hair back in a ponytail with a red and white striped ribbon. She looked as beautiful as when he'd taken her to the winery two nights earlier, and she'd worn a burgundy dress and heels.

"You look beautiful," he remarked, bending to give her a slow kiss.

Macy felt her knees go a little weak. "Thank you," she whispered. "You look pretty terrific yourself. I like the team shirt you're wearing."

"It's like the one the coaching staff wears," he said proudly. "Makes me look more official as the team doctor, don't you think?"

"Definitely," she agreed, handing him her keys so he could lock her door. They stepped off her front porch just as Chandler and Peter were coming from Chandler's house.

"Hello, there," Macy greeted them. "Is Rosie coming with you tonight?"

"Yep," Chandler answered. "We're headed there now. She thought it best if we drove, though, since the stadium is a little farther than she'd want to walk. I just hope we can find a parking space up close."

Jake had a solution to that issue. "I have a designated place up front that I'm not going to use. I'll tell the boosters manning the entrance that you'll be parking there in my place."

"That would be great!" Chandler exclaimed. "You don't think they'll have an issue since we don't have a pass or anything?"

"You'll have Rosie in the car. I think that's the only kind of pass you'll need," he answered. Jake knew that Rosie was this town's version of royalty, and everyone knew her. "We'll see you at the game."

"Sounds good," Peter said. "And save us some good seats too!" The last was shouted out of the open car window as they drove up the street.

Jake took Macy's hand, and they made their way to the football stadium. Even though they had been to the scrimmage the week before, this was a whole new experience. Macy could smell the popcorn in the concession stand and hear the band warming up in the parking lot. As they walked by the booster parents working in the parking lot, Jake told them Rosie would be using his spot. As he suspected, it was no problem.

They continued walking on past the cheerleading squad. Some were stretching, and others were making sure their hair and makeup were perfect. They all had matching red bows on perfectly done ponytails. Macy recognized the two girls who had been in the bakery a few weeks back. As they walked by, she heard one of them say, "Look, there's Dr. Grainger. That must be the nurse Cody's mom was talking about. I don't think she's cute at all!"

Macy was close to stopping and saying something to the girl when Jake squeezed her hand. She looked up to find him smiling at her. "So, I'm dating a cute nurse, huh?"

"Apparently, it depends on whether you're asking a mom or a teenager," she said, laughing.

"I agree with the mom," he remarked, putting his arm around her. They continued walking up to the ticket booth. As Jake was about to purchase two tickets, they realized that Cody's mom was behind the counter.

"Oh, no, Dr. Grainger, you and Macy are our medical staff, so you get in free," she explained. "Enjoy the game," she said, with a wink and a smile toward Macy. Macy just smiled and rolled her eyes.

As they walked up onto the running track that surrounded the field, Macy continued to take it all in. Having never gone to an actual game before, she found the whole scene fascinating. Both teams were on opposite sides of the field. She could see that some of the players were stretching, the kickers looked to be practicing field goals, and others were practicing plays. Fortunately, even though she'd never been to a game, she loved watching it on television, so she knew what was going on.

They continued across the track to let the coaching staff know they were there. After meeting the athletic trainer that the county provided on a part-time basis, they made their way to the concession stand. Macy took in all the smells coming from the building. The boosters looked like a well-oiled machine, with the dads cooking hot dogs and hamburgers on the commercial-grade grills and the moms working at the counters.

"Okay, I promised you a three-course dinner, so what do you want for your appetizer, dinner, and dessert?" Jake asked Macy as they looked up at the menu painted on a large board across the front of the stand.

"I think I'll start with popcorn since I've smelled it since we arrived," Macy told him. She saw something she didn't quite recognize. "Do you know what a taco-in-a-bag is?"

Jake laughed, "Haven't a clue." He turned to the mom behind the counter. "Can you explain what the taco-in-a-bag is?"

The mom laughed and explained that it was a large bag of corn chips with a big helping of chili and cheese dumped inside the bag, topped with shredded lettuce. "Hence the name taco-in-a-bag."

Jake looked to Macy. "I'm game if you are," she said. She figured she could have a hot dog or hamburger at the diner, but where else could she experience such a culinary masterpiece.

"Alright, then, we'll have two boxes of popcorn, two taco-in-a-bag things." He turned back to Macy. "Dessert?"

"Chocolate chip cookies," she answered. She knew for a fact that Sweet Stuff Bakery donated the cookies, and they would be outstanding.

"Add four chocolate chip cookies and two colas, and we should be good for the game," Jake told the mom. After paying for their three-course dinner and getting a box to carry everything in, they headed up toward their seats.

The bleachers were set up above the field by about five feet, so even the first row could see over the cheerleaders standing on the track. "Let's go about halfway up and on an end so we can get to the field in a hurry if we need to," Jake said as they made their way down the walkway. He also wanted to be on the fifty-yard line.

They were just getting settled in when Peter, Chandler, and Rosie arrived. "Yum, taco-in-a-bag!" Chandler said excitedly, "I haven't had that in such a long time!"

Rosie looked at the box they were holding. "Looks like you have a five-star, three-course dinner there," she said, referring to the comment Macy had made to Myrtle the night before. "The best you can get at a football game, that's for sure," she remarked, smiling. "Peter, I think I'll have the same if you don't mind."

"No problem, Grandmother." He loved making his grandmother happy. "Chandler, do you want to come and help me carry everything?"

"Sure thing," Chandler replied. "We'll be right back."

"And you were smart to get everything all at once," Rosie told Jake. "Once the game starts, you'd miss half of it waiting in line. Not because of slow service either, but because this place will be packed."

"How many games have you come to?" Macy asked Rosie.

Rosie smiled proudly. "Unless it's raining or really cold, I haven't missed a game since I was little."

Jake looked at Rosie with a shocked expression. "Are you serious? Rosie, I had no idea you loved football."

"There's a lot about me you don't know," Rosie told the pair with a sly grin. "But, yes, I love sports. That's why, if a sports bar happens to open in Hope Springs, you might just find me there watching a game or two. I don't drink alcohol, but I love watching with other people and feeling the energy around."

"That's so interesting," Macy told her.

When Peter and Chandler came back with their dinner, Jake asked, "Peter, did you know Rosie was such a sports fan?"

Peter looked at a smiling Rosie. "Seriously?" Rosie just nodded her head.

"Oh, you're one of those closet fans who watch with the shades closed, so no one sees you," Peter joked.

Rosie just slapped him on the arm. "I do no such thing! I'm more than willing to admit to anyone who asks that I like sports."

"She even said she'd go to a sports bar to watch games," Macy informed them. "Peter, you should think about opening one up in one of your new buildings."

"You know, that might not be a bad idea," Jake agreed. "Know anyone who'd want to invest in one?"

"Not off the top of my head," Peter answered. "And the way the plans are now, there isn't room for one in either of the new buildings. Too bad there isn't a vacant storefront on Main Street."

By now, more of their friends had filed in, including Hillary and Jack Smith and their children. "Why are you looking for a storefront?" Jack asked, handing one of his kids a juice box.

"We were talking about how nice it would be to have a sports bar in Hope Springs," Macy told them, taking a bite of her taco-in-a-bag. "You know, this is actually good."

"I know, taco-in-a-bag is the best junk food," Chandler agreed, taking a bite of her own.

"I happen to know that a storefront is going to be up for sale by the end of November," Jack said. "Mr. Thompson is retiring and closing the hardware store. He told me today that he can't get any of his kids to take it over, so he's just going to close it. It's in a great location between the bakery and the Hilltop. Of course, the church is one block behind, so I'm not sure how they'd feel about a bar being so close."

"Well, it's a shame that Jim couldn't get any of his kids to run the business, but I don't see why the church would care if it's a respectable business. Maybe something more family and community-oriented than just a bar," Rosie told the group.

"Yeah," Chandler agreed, excitedly, "a place where anyone can feel comfortable having dinner, maybe with town sports memorabilia on the walls, from little league on up. There could be flat-screen televisions around, and a bar, but also booths and tables as well."

Peter took in everyone's comments. He could see the potential of investing in such a place for the town. Now, to get the investors. "Let me think about this and talk to Mr. Thompson to see what his asking price is going to be. Not a bad idea, though."

As more fans began filling the stands on both sides, Macy looked around and saw that the Advice Quilting Bee members and their families were all around them. Apparently, Rosie wasn't the only one who loved sports. Myrtle was decked out in Hope Springs sports attire and colors from her head to her toes. Fran chose to wear a peasant blouse and long skirt in team colors. Hillary's son was wearing a miniature Hope Springs football uniform, and her daughter made the cutest little mini-cheerleader. *This is what small town is really like,* Macy thought to herself, *and I love it.*

Later, as the game clock ticked to zero and the scoreboard reflected that Hope Springs had won twenty-eight to twenty-one on a last-second touchdown, Macy couldn't remember loving an evening more. She and the others had cheered until they were hoarse, and the home team didn't disappoint. And luckily, Jake's services as the team doctor weren't needed. No injuries on either side.

She and Jake walked with the masses down Main Street, folks turning off left and right when they got to their street. They continued down past Jake's street, and since it was such a lovely evening, past Macy's street as well. Walking hand in hand, Macy didn't want the night to end. They strolled along the lake, all lit up by the full moon. When Jake stopped and turned to take Macy in his arms for a kiss, she didn't resist. She'd waited all night for this moment.

"I kind of like where this is going," Jake whispered as he raised his head, not letting her out of his embrace.

"I kind of like it myself," Macy agreed, smiling. And she silently prayed this feeling would never go away but knew that eventually, reality would come back with a vengeance.

They walked on to Macy's house, where Jake made sure she was safely inside before making his way to his own home.

As he entered, he remembered leaving dishes in the sink as he hurried out to the game. He walked into the kitchen and turned on the light. "Really?!" he said sarcastically. He opened the dishwasher door, and there, inside, were the very dishes he'd left in the sink. "Thanks, Maggie," he said, smiling as he turned off the light and went to bed.

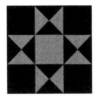

Chapter 25

The month of September seemed to fly. Macy and Jake began cooking dinner together each night, and if the day had been hectic, they'd go to the diner. Thursday nights, of course, Macy would go to the Advice Quilting Bee, and Jake would be on his own. Friday nights, they went to the football games, both home and away. Saturday mornings, Jake would go on his runs, and Macy would spend the morning catching up on errands, laundry, and housework. She wasn't sure when Jake accomplished those tasks but figured he must.

The rest of the time, they were together visiting historical sights and other places in Virginia neither had gone to or spending time with Chandler and Peter. By the end of the month, it was pretty well known that Jake and Macy were a couple.

On the last Saturday of September, the town held a welcome home celebration for Katrina Smith. Rosie and Myrtle presented her with the star quilt made by the ladies of the Advice Quilting Bee. Katrina carefully rubbed her hand over the quilt, and with tears streaming down her face, thanked the ladies for their beautiful creation. Rosie hugged her and told her the ladies of the Advice Quilting Bee were there for her. Andrea held a small reception for all the attendees at the diner afterward, where Katrina's parents thanked all for their love, prayers, and support in bringing their daughter home safely.

That evening, as Jake and Macy were sitting on the loveseat on her front porch, they talked about how brave Katrina had been. "I honestly don't think I could have done what she's done," Macy admitted.

"She certainly has been to hell and back," Jake concurred. "She brought me her medical records and authorization to treat her. Her body has been through so many traumas. But I'm more concerned about her state of mind. I told her if she needs to talk, we're here."

"Absolutely," Macy agreed. "She has to be going through PTSD."

"She has her parents, too. And having a father who is a counselor will help. But sometimes, the family is too close to a situation to notice subtle changes. I cautioned them about that," he said.

Macy shook her head in agreement. In that regard, she knew Katrina was more fortunate than she had been. "She is lucky to have them."

"I'd like to think that if I'd been in that position, my parents would have been there for me," Jake stated. Macy felt the conversation shift to a topic she wasn't ready to discuss. "I know they would have been. They were wonderful parents who raised me in a loving environment. My mom was a room mother in my elementary school, and my dad was one of my scout leaders, pushing me to Eagle," he said, smiling.

"Pushing you?" Macy asked. What she would have given to have had parents like that.

"Yeah, by the time I got to high school, I was kind of done with scouts, but my father was an Eagle Scout, and he

176

knew that I'd regret it if I didn't achieve such an honor, having been so close," he explained. "He was right, of course, and I finished before my junior year of high school. Now I can proudly say I'm an Eagle Scout. And maybe, someday, my son can be one as well."

Jake let that last statement hang in the air. He and Macy had never really discussed anything beyond the now, but once he said it, Jake realized that he wanted a family and was pretty sure he wanted it with Macy. He could tell from her body language that there was something not quite right with the direction of the conversation. Then he remembered he didn't know anything about her family.

"Macy?" Jake asked, looking straight ahead. "Tell me about your family."

Macy started to shift uncomfortably next to Jake. Her breathing came in quick, short breaths, almost like she was having a panic attack. She wasn't sure what to tell him, but the truth was not it. She hated to lie to Jake but figured if he knew the truth, that she was the daughter of two drug-addicted parents, he'd judge her differently, and it would forever change their relationship.

So, she lied, sort of. "My parents passed away when I was little." *There, that wasn't so hard,* Macy thought. She didn't think there was any need to elaborate.

Jake could sense there was more to the story but thought it best to let the subject rest for now. He knew that Macy had taken a considerable step in telling him that much, and he wanted to make sure she knew she could trust and count on him. Jake did the only thing he could think of; he put his arm around her, kissed her on the cheek, and held her. He hoped she could feel his love wrap around her like the quilt they had presented to Katrina earlier in the evening. He felt her breathing slow and knew that she was finally relaxing.

Macy was glad that Jake didn't ask any questions. She knew it would be harder to lie the next time. And as they sat there with her enclosed in his embrace, Macy knew that it would be only a matter of time before she'd have to tell him everything. She just hoped that they would be so much in love that it wouldn't matter by then. Macy had never been in love. The affair, which Jake also didn't know about, wasn't real love. *Oh God, too many secrets and too many lies!* Macy thought, her breathing increasing again. She felt Jake tighten his hold on her. She took a deep breath and decided to let it all go, for now.

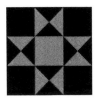

Chapter 26

"So, how are the plans for the wedding coming?" Rosie asked Chandler as they sat quilting on Thursday evening. "Only a month to go, right?"

"Yes, and I can't believe it," Chandler said, smiling a huge smile. "It seems like only yesterday we were all standing around this very frame, and Peter was proposing to me. It's gone by so fast, and then again, not fast enough."

"Yeah," Myrtle agreed, putting her needle down and taking off her reading glasses. "And soon we may be planning another wedding," she added, looking at Macy.

Macy chose to keep her head down and focus on her section of the Christmas quilt they were working on. She wasn't sure where Myrtle got her information, but she thought that assumption was way too premature.

Fran picked up on Macy's hesitance to comment. "Now, Myrtle, let's get through one wedding before we're planning another one when the poor child isn't even engaged. We don't want to scare him off, do we?" Where Myrtle was one to say whatever was on her mind, Fran was the more sensible and compassionate one.

"Yeah, I thought we were going leave Macy alone," Hillary added, feeling the need to stick up for her friend.

Rosie, ever the voice of reason, said, "Myrtle, I think Jake has made his feelings for Macy quite clear. I don't feel it's necessary to put the cart before the horse." She turned to Macy. "Macy, if you want to say something, that's fine. If you don't, then we'll all respect your privacy."

Macy gave them all a weak smile. On the one hand, she did need someone to talk to about what had happened on her front porch the other night. On the other hand, if all these people knew about her secrets, it might get back to Jake before Macy was ready to talk to him, and that would be the end of life as she knew it. But she did need someone's advice. The indecision must have shown on her face.

"If you ever need to talk to us, you know we're here for you," Rosie told her. "Whenever."

"Thank you," Macy said quietly.

"Okay, ladies, back to work," Rosie ordered the group.

As the evening wore on, Macy focused less and less on her stitching. Chandler must have noticed because when Macy got up to get a drink, Chandler followed.

"Is everything okay?" Chandler asked.

Macy took a sip of water. "Of course, why do you ask?" She tried to sound convincing.

"When you go back to your spot, take a look at your stitches," Chandler told her.

"That bad, huh?"

Chandler made a zig-zag motion through the air with her finger.

Macy walked back to her spot at the frame. She saw that she had, indeed, stitched an entire row entirely off the line Mary Ann had carefully drawn for them to follow. She was going to have to remove the stitches. An hour's worth of work wasted. And then came the tears. She backed away from the quilt so she didn't drop any on the beautiful fabric, but the tears wouldn't stop. "I'm so sorry, I've ruined the quilt," she apologized through the flood of tears.

Chandler came to her side with tissues. "You didn't ruin it, honey. It will be fine. We can remove these with no problem," Chandler looked around at the others with a pleading look.

"Absolutely," Hillary said. "Do you know how many stitches I've had to remove because I went off the line? Thousands." She got up to stand on Macy's other side. "Maybe you should call it quits for tonight." She looked at the others in the group. "And none of us will speak of this ever again," she said forcefully, looking directly at Myrtle.

"Of course, we won't," Myrtle assured Macy as she stood beside Macy's work. "I'll get these stitches removed in a jiffy."

"Chandler, why don't you and Macy call it a night," Rosie recommended. "We're almost done here anyway." Rosie knew there was something big going on, and she guessed that Macy didn't want the whole group to know. She hoped that Chandler could somehow get Macy to open up so they'd know how to help her.

"That sounds like a great idea," Chandler agreed. "Get your things, Macy, and we'll walk home."

Macy gave Myrtle and Rosie each a hug and told Mary Ann again how sorry she was for messing up. "Don't you worry about it," Mary Ann said, hugging her. "We'll fix it, and you won't even know it happened. You go on home and get some rest."

Macy allowed Chandler to lead her out of Rosie's and on back to her house. Chandler took Macy's keys from her and unlocked the front door. As they walked inside, Macy walked back to her kitchen and got a bottle of Merlot and two glasses. "Come on, let's go to the front porch," she said, referring to the front porch talks they had when there was something significant to discuss.

"Alright," Chandler followed, noticing that it was only nine-thirty.

Macy poured them each a glass, and they sat on the same loveseat she and Jake had been on earlier in the week. "So, Jake started talking all about his parents and what a loving household he grew up in and how he was an Eagle Scout, for goodness sake!" she all but shouted. "How can I possibly live up to that?!" She took a big drink of her wine, letting the cool liquid calm her nerves. "There's no way I deserve an Eagle Scout." And the tears started again.

"My goodness," Chandler began. "What makes you think you don't deserve an Eagle Scout? You are by far the kindest, warm, loving, and genuine person I know. You deserve someone like Jake."

Macy just shook her head from side to side. She wagged her finger at Chandler. "No, you don't know me. You think you do, but you really don't." She took another gulp of wine to try and calm her nerves. The first one hadn't worked.

"Oh, big deal, so you had an affair with your employer," Chandler said like that was something done every day.

"No, that's not the only thing," Macy admitted. "I'm the product of two drug addicts, Chandler! I never had the loving home that Jake had. And, worse, I lied to him," she cried, ashamed of such a thing. "I lied to an Eagle Scout!" More tears and another gulp of wine.

Chandler was trying hard not to laugh at how incredibly ironic that statement was. She was sure there was something in the scout oath about them not telling lies. "Honey, you aren't an Eagle Scout, Jake is," she said, trying to say something that might make Macy laugh, just a little. Or at the very least stop crying.

It worked. Macy stopped and looked at her friend, then she started laughing so hard that she almost started crying again. Putting the glass up to her lips for another drink, she realized it was empty. Chandler refilled it and her own. Macy drank more. Chandler figured she was getting up the courage to divulge the lie. She was.

"Okay, here goes," Macy said. "I told him my parents died when I was little." She held up her hand to Chandler, and in a somewhat drunk voice, said, "I know, I know, it was terrible to tell that kind of lie, especially after what happened with your parents," referring to the fact that Chandler's parents had died in a car accident when she was young. "But in reality, it's only a partial lie. Please don't be mad at me."

"I'm not mad at you, sweetie. And what do you mean that it's only a partial lie?"

Macy took another gulp of wine, thinking she probably shouldn't be drinking so much. She did, after all, have to work the next day, and then there was a home football game that night. "I'm going to regret drinking this much in the morning, aren't I?" she asked Chandler.

Chandler smiled. "Probably. What do you mean by 'partial lie'?" Chandler wanted her to keep talking so she could figure out what this whole episode was about.

"Technically, my dad is really dead," Macy told her, acting proud that she'd told the truth. "But not my mom."

Chandler was more than a little confused. "What do you mean 'technically'? Is he in a coma or on life support somewhere? I don't understand?"

Macy shook her drunken head from side to side. "Oh, not a good idea. Now the front porch is spinning." She sat back against the back of the couch. "Okay, it's stopped. No, he's dead and buried...somewhere." She added the 'somewhere' a little late.

What does she mean, 'somewhere?' Chandler got a little worried. Did she kill him, bury him, and not remember where? "Macy, honey, did you do something to your dad?" she asked carefully.

Macy just stared at her and then started laughing. "What?! Of course not. He died in prison when I was ten years old. I have no idea where he's buried."

"Prison?" Chandler asked, clearly not following her drunk friend very well. "Macy, I think I need for you to start from the beginning." Chandler was so confused, and they hadn't even gotten to what happened to her mother yet. As Macy tried to take another gulp of wine, Chandler took the glass from her hand. "No, I think we've had enough of this," she said as she put the glass on the small side table.

Macy, not too happy that Chandler took away her nerve-calming liquid, finally said, "Okay, I'll tell you the whole thing, and then you'll understand why I'm not good enough for an Eagle Scout. I mean, Jake." Macy took a deep breath

184

and then began telling Chandler everything about her lousy parents, and the lousy foster homes she'd been in, and how she had to do everything for herself.

"I'm not sure where my mom is now and I don't care. The last time I saw her, all she wanted was money for more drugs. I told her I wasn't going to be an enabler. She got mad, told me I was a brat and left. That was two years ago, right after I graduated with my nursing degree. I was so proud of what I'd done, and she couldn't care less! All she wanted was money for drugs!"

Chandler sat, letting Macy tell her story without interruption. When she'd finished, Chandler put her arm around her and handed her more tissues. "Thank you for trusting me enough to tell me all this. But now I have something to tell you, and I mean this with the utmost respect," Chandler told her best friend. "I think you're an idiot!"

"What!?!" Macy yelled. "Why am I an idiot?!" She'd just poured her heart out to her best friend, and she had the nerve to call her an idiot?

"You, my dearest friend, don't give yourself enough credit. You've risen beyond anyone's expectations, from your parents to your foster parents, even to that stupid doctor you'd worked for in the city. You are so much better than any of them. And you did it all on your own," Chandler explained. "I'm so proud of you, and I think Jake would be too."

"Do you think so?" Macy asked, insecurity setting in. "I don't know if I can tell him all that I've told you yet." *At least not sober,* Macy mused.

As if reading her mind, Chandler smiled and pointed to the empty Merlot bottle. "Maybe you shouldn't be drinking when you talk to him."

"Good point," Macy agreed. "So, you think I'm making too much of this?" She needed Chandler's reassurance on this one.

"Yes, I do," Chandler knew Macy well enough to know that positive reinforcement was the best way to go. "I think you owe him at least the truth on what happened with your parents. Unfortunately, he'll want to know the whole story, but he may also be understanding enough to let you tell him the whole thing in your own time. I just wouldn't wait too long."

"Thanks for being such a good friend," Macy said, hugging Chandler close. "I'll take your advice under consideration. But for now, I think it's time for bed." Once Chandler had made it safely across the street, Macy went into her own home. She knew what Chandler said made sense, but right now, she was exhausted and just wanted to crawl into bed.

Chapter 27

The next morning Macy woke feeling like she'd been hit by a Mack truck. She slowly opened her eyes, but the sunlight peeking through the shades seemed to be blinding her, so Macy closed her eyes again. Remembering the only yoga class she took, the instructor mentioned something about lying still and checking in with her body, so she did that. From what she could tell, everything seemed to be working okay. She could move her arms and legs, although all felt like they had lead weights on them.

She realized in the checking-in process that her bladder was also working correctly, so she decided she'd better get up soon or risk having to change her sheets. *How much wine did I have?* She couldn't remember.

As she slowly pulled back the covers and swung her legs off the side of the bed to a sitting position, Macy realized she had a big problem. The room began to spin, and a wave of nausea hit her full force. She lay back down with her legs still dangling off the side.

I don't remember a hangover ever feeling like this, Macy thought. But she knew she had to get to the bathroom, so she made another attempt to sit up, this time a little slower.

"Okay, this is a little better," she said out loud, waiting for the wave to hit.

When she felt like she would be okay, she slowly put her feet on the carpeted floor and made her way to a standing position. "Not too bad." Not wanting to take the chance of having any kind of accident, Macy hurried to the bathroom.

After, as she was washing her hands, Macy looked at herself in the mirror. "Oh, Lord," she groaned. It was then that the wave of nausea returned. She was glad she was already in the bathroom because she probably wouldn't have made it otherwise.

When Macy finally finished praying to the porcelain gods, she splashed cold water on her face. Looking again in the mirror, she realized she had absolutely no color. Then the chills started. Macy placed her hand on her forehead. She was burning up with fever. "Okay, I've had hangovers before, and not once have I ever had a fever." She slowly made her way back to her bedroom with energy she didn't have and crawled back into bed.

The next time Macy woke up, it was to the sound of someone banging, very loudly, on her front door. It took every ounce of energy she had to look at her clock—eleven o'clock in the morning. "What?!" she cried. Feeling so crummy, she didn't even care that she was late for work.

The constant banging continued, but not having the energy to get up, she reached for her phone on her bedside table and saw that she'd missed calls from Chandler, the medical center, and Jake. Knowing Chandler had a key to her place, she called her.

Without even a hello first, Chandler screamed into the phone, "Macy, are you alright!?" She was frantic.

"No. Too weak to answer door. Someone pounding. Make them stop." And that was about all the energy Macy had.

"On my way!" Chandler yelled before she hung up.

Macy didn't even have the energy to put the phone back on the bedside table before she was back to sleep.

Sometime later, she had no idea when, Macy woke to the sound of voices quietly talking in her living room. She vaguely remembered calling Chandler. At some point, and this may have been a dream, Jake took her temperature and gave her medicine. She needed to use the bathroom again, but after her last attempt, she felt it best if she had help getting there this time.

"Chandler," Macy called out in the loudest voice she could muster. Clearly, that wasn't loud enough because no one came running. *Alright,* she thought, reaching for her phone. *This is one of those times when technology comes in handy.* She texted a simple, straightforward message to Chandler: HELP BATHROOM.

The next thing Macy knew, both Chandler and Jake were standing beside her bed. "Hey, guys, what brings you to my humble abode?" she asked, trying to be witty.

"Macy Greenburg, you had the whole town worried," Chandler scolded her. "You wouldn't answer your phone or your door."

Macy was too weak to be apologetic. "Bathroom, now," was all she said in response.

"Okay, let's get you up slowly, so you don't black out," Jake instructed, pulling back her covers. Macy was silently thankful she wore pajamas to bed. "You're still burning up with fever," Jake astutely noticed. "Once we get you up and Chandler helps you to the bathroom, I'll get you something for that. The flu medicine didn't do much yet."

"Flu?" Macy asked quizzically. She knew she was sick, but not that sick.

"Yes, honey, Jake said you have the flu," Chandler spoke to her like she was a child.

"Did you get the flu vaccine?" Jake asked, sounding more like her doctor and less like her boyfriend.

Macy shook her head 'no'. Even that hurt. "Did I infect anyone else?"

As Chandler helped her inch her way to the bathroom, she told her that everyone at the Advice Quilting Bee had gotten their flu shot.

"Good," Macy answered before closing the bathroom door.

Jake looked at his watch and saw that he needed to get back to the medical center. They had been able to cancel the morning appointments, but there were some afternoon patients to see. Then he had to go to the football game. Luckily it was a home game. "I'll give her this dose of medicine and then go," he told Chandler as they waited for Macy to emerge from the bathroom.

"Don't worry. I can stay with her." Chandler wasn't about to leave her best friend alone.

Once they got Macy tucked back into bed, and Jake gave her something to bring the fever down, he kissed Macy on the forehead. "I'll be back after the game." But Macy was already back to sleep.

As Chandler walked Jake out to the front door, Jake told her to watch for any signs of delirium, her fever going higher, rapid breathing, or anything else unusual. "If there is any change, call nine-one-one and then me," he instructed her.

"Is it that serious?" Chandler asked, worry written all over her face.

"I'm only concerned that we haven't been able to bring the fever down," he explained, "Hopefully, this last dose will do the trick. Next time she wakes up, see if you can get some liquids in her."

"Okay. I'll text you when she wakes up and give you an update," Chandler assured him. After Jake left, Chandler closed the door and sent a silent prayer to the Heavens that her best friend would be okay.

The fever medicine must have worked because Macy woke up completely soaked in sweat a few hours later. And while she was still weak, she did have enough strength to get out of bed and find Chandler. "I think I need help changing the sheets," she stated in a weak voice. "I'm guessing my fever broke."

Chandler jumped up from the couch and helped Macy back down the hall. "Do you want to try and take a shower and maybe get some of the sweat off?"

"That would probably be a good idea," Macy agreed. "I have clean pajamas in the top dresser drawer, and there are clean sheets in the hall closet."

"I'll take care of it," Chandler assured her. "You go get in the shower, and I'll bring you clean clothes."

Macy stripped off her sweaty pajamas and turned the water on, letting the steam warm the bathroom. She checked to make sure the temperature wasn't too hot, stepped into the tub, and drew the shower curtain closed. Standing under the spray, letting the water rinse all the sickness and sweat from her skin, she was feeling a little better. *Maybe I'm going to live, after all,* she thought as she washed and conditioned her hair.

After using her favorite honeysuckle body wash to take care of the rest, Macy pulled back the curtain and reached for a towel. She wrapped her long hair in it and then grabbed another to dry her body. Dressed in clean pajamas, she unwrapped her hair and began combing the long tresses. Macy opened the bathroom door to let the steam escape and decided it might be best to dry her hair rather than go back to bed with wet hair.

As she reached under the sink for her blow dryer, the room began to spin. She sat down on the toilet and waited for the episode to pass. "Chandler," Macy called, realizing she was going to need help with the task. "Would you mind helping me dry my hair? I tried but started to get lightheaded."

"Absolutely. I have your bed all made, and the dirty sheets are in the washer," Chandler said as she reached under the sink to retrieve the blow dryer. "Do you want to come out and sit at the kitchen table while I dry your hair? I could make you some tea and toast if you're up to it."

Macy realized she hadn't had anything to eat in almost twenty-four hours, and other than water to take her medicine, she hadn't had anything to drink either. "Tea and toast would be great," Macy said with a tired smile. She realized that just the act of taking a shower had taken a lot out of her. She followed Chandler out into the kitchen.

As Macy sat watching Chandler make her toast and tea, she thought about how lucky she was to have such good friends. It took a special person to come and stay with her, change her dirty sheets, make her tea and toast, and blow-dry her hair. "Thank you," she told Chandler. "I don't know what I did to deserve such a good friend, but I'm so glad you're here."

Chandler put the tea and toast on the table in front of Macy and hugged her. "Oh, honey, I'm sure you'd do the same for me. God brought you here to Hope Springs, and I'm so glad He did." She picked up the blow dryer and plugged it in. "Now you eat while I play hairdresser."

After her hair was dry and she'd had the cup of tea and the toast, it was all Macy could do to stay awake. "This flu is sapping my energy," she said, yawning. "I think I'm going to go back to bed. You don't have to stay anymore; I think I can handle things from here."

"Oh, no," Chandler insisted. "Jake told me not to leave you alone, and I'm listening to the doctor. I texted him while you were in the shower to let him know your fever had broken, but he said I should still stay with you in case it comes back."

Macy only vaguely remembered Jake being there earlier. "Okay, you're in luck. I don't have the energy to argue." Macy climbed back into bed and promptly fell asleep.

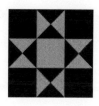

Chapter 28

Once again, the light shining in Macy's eyes woke her up the following day. *I'm going to have to get better shades,* she thought, rubbing her eyes and stretching. She looked across the room and saw that Jake had arrived sometime during the night and fell asleep in her chair. She took a moment to look at him. Still dressed in his Hope Springs football team shirt and blue jeans, he looked devastatingly handsome with his wavy, light brown hair falling across his forehead. *How could someone look drop-dead gorgeous while sleeping?* she thought to herself as she brushed her hair off her face.

Jake woke to see Macy looking at him with her big blue eyes and didn't think he'd ever seen anything more beautiful. Even sick with the flu, she was still breathtaking. "Hi," he said quietly. "How are you feeling?"

Macy wiggled her fingers and toes and then her arms and legs. "Not achy anymore," she replied, smiling. "Guess I'm going to survive." Now that she was more coherent, Macy was aware of the intimate situation they found themselves in. She was, after all, in her pajamas. Oh well, too late for modesty now.

"Can I get you some tea or something to eat?" he asked, a bit unsure of what to do now that he was here and she was awake. Jake wanted nothing more than to take her in his arms and tell her how worried he'd been for the past two days, but something held him back.

Macy stretched and smiled. "That sounds great. I'm actually hungry." Other than the one piece of toast she'd had the night before, she hadn't eaten anything since Thursday night. "Let me use the bathroom and splash some water on my face, and I'll meet you in the kitchen." She waited until Jake left the room and then retrieved her robe from the hook on the back of the door and went to the bathroom.

A few minutes later, Macy walked into the kitchen to find Jake serving up cinnamon toast and tea. "I don't think I've ever had cinnamon toast," she told him as she sat down at the table.

"Really?! I thought that was the first rule of motherhood—learning to make cinnamon toast." He then recalled that she had mentioned her parents had died. "I'm sorry," he apologized.

"No, it's okay," she assured him. "Not everyone was lucky enough to grow up with loving parents." She knew that this was probably her opening to confess and tell him the truth. She took a bite of her toast. "This is delicious!" *Okay, quit stalling. You have to tell him the truth,* she told herself. She looked down at her hands in her lap. "Jake, there's something I have to tell you, and I don't think you're going to like it."

Jake had known all week there was something Macy was holding back. He was glad that she was finally going to let it out so they could deal with it. "Okay," he said hesitantly.

"My parents aren't really dead, or at least my mom isn't...I don't think." There, she said it.

Jake sat there playing with his napkin. "I'm not sure I understand. Maybe you should start from the beginning." First, they were dead, and then they weren't dead, then only her dad was dead, she thought? What did that mean? He was trying not to get angry over the fact that she'd lied. He didn't want to say or do something that would cause her to stop telling him everything.

Macy took a sip of her tea and put the cup back in the saucer. "Okay, but please don't interrupt until I'm finished because I don't think I could tell this more than once."

He shook his head, letting her know he understood.

"I wasn't as fortunate as you in the parent department. My parents were both drug addicts. Luckily, I didn't have any of the effects of being born to a mother who was an addict. Guess God figured my life would be hard enough without having to go through that as well," she explained with a wry smile.

After taking another sip of tea, she continued. "When I was six, my father was arrested for dealing drugs. My mom was an addict and in no condition to care for a child. We had no other family, so I was placed in the foster care system. My foster parents, of whom there were many, weren't much better than my parents. While I was never abused, all the money they received that was supposed to go to caring for me went into their pockets.

"By the time I got to high school, I'd lived in more places than I could count. Fortunately, during high school, I only lived in two foster homes, and they were both in the same school district. I was lucky enough to have a great counselor who mentored me all the way through. I also worked in the evenings and put all my extra money in the bank. I knew the only way to survive was to care for myself and make sure I had a career in mind. Since I got straight

A's in high school, I received a full scholarship to nursing school. So, the money I'd saved I used for rent once I graduated and turned eighteen."

She stopped and drank some more tea. Jake thought she was finished, so he asked, "What happened to your parents?"

"My father died in prison, and I don't even know where he's buried," she said sadly.

"And your mom?"

"Mom...," she said with a sarcastic laugh. "Well, the last I heard from her was two years ago when I graduated from college. She came to see me. She said she'd seen an article in the paper announcing the graduates and saw my name." Jake noticed her hands start to shake and tears welling up in her eyes. He put his hand on hers, letting her know he was there for her. "She didn't come to congratulate me or tell me how proud she was of me," she quietly explained, wiping tears from her cheeks. "No, she wanted money for more drugs."

"And what did you do?" Jake hoped she hadn't given in to her because that was a cycle that he'd seen in his residency that was hard to break.

Macy looked up at him and proudly said, "I told her no!" Jake released a breath he hadn't realized he was holding. "She told me I was a disgrace of a child and walked out. I haven't seen her since."

"Thank you," Jake said, squeezing her hand.

Macy looked at him with tear-filled eyes. "For what?"

"For telling me the truth," he said.

Macy laughed a cynical laugh. "Oh, but wait, there's more. I also had an affair with my previous employer!" There, she blurted it out. Can't take it back now. She waited for Jake to get up and walk out of her life. But instead, he continued holding her hand and not squeezing it, just holding it gently.

"I know," he told her.

"You know?!" How could he possibly know?

"Honey, I did my residency in the same hospital where he had patients. Nurses talked. They said something about him using his new nurse to get back at his wife for having an affair with his partner. When I saw your resume, I realized it was the same practice. When Rosie mentioned you had said you came to Hope Springs to work for an older doctor, I figured it out."

Macy covered her face in her hands. "I'm so humiliated," she groaned.

"Macy, please don't be embarrassed," he tried to reassure her. "That jerk used you to get back at his wife. And after hearing what you've just told me, honey, you were just looking for someone to love you. I can understand that."

Macy couldn't believe she could be so lucky. "You're sure? You're not upset that I didn't tell you the truth about my parents. And you're not upset that I had an affair?"

Jake took both her hands in his. "No one in this world is perfect. Would I have liked for you to have felt comfortable enough to tell me the truth the other night? Yes. But that doesn't make me love you any less."

Macy's hearing must have been affected by the flu. "You love me?" she asked, hoping she'd heard correctly.

"Yes, I do. And I'm hoping the feeling is mutual," he answered, smiling.

Macy wrapped her arms around his neck. "Yes, I love you, too! And I promise no more secrets!"

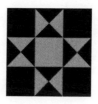

Chapter 29

By Wednesday, Macy was finally feeling more like her old self. She managed to make it through a full day of work but crashed when she got home. Jake was kind enough to bring her dinner from the diner.

Thursday morning, she couldn't believe how much better she felt. That evening, going into Rosie's for the Advice Quilting Bee, it was hard to believe it had only been a week since her meltdown at the last meeting. So much had happened in such a short time. Not the least of which was the fact that she and Jake had declared their love for one another.

As the ladies assembled around the quilt frame after dinner, Macy noticed that the stitching that she had done so horribly the week before had been removed, and someone had done beautiful stitches in their place.

"Thank you to whoever fixed my mess from the last week," Macy said quietly, touching the stitching carefully like it was a fine painting. She looked around the table at her wonderful group of friends. "I feel I owe all of you an apology for my behavior last week. I don't know what came over me."

"You have nothing for which you need to apologize," Rosie said reassuringly. "What happened last week is one of the main reasons we're here, to support one another through good and bad."

Myrtle moved to hug Macy. "Yes, it is. If one of us needs help or support, we all know who to call."

"Exactly," Chandler agreed. "Just like when you were too sick to answer the door, you called me."

Macy smiled a shy smile. "I knew you had a key to my house and could come and make the person stop banging on my door. I had no idea that person was Jake."

"We're just happy you survived the flu," Andrea told her. "Not that I minded Jake getting take out for you every night."

"He was so worried about you, Macy," Rosie said. "It was very evident his feelings were genuine and true. And we couldn't be happier for you both."

Everyone agreed that Macy and Jake were so good for each other. Macy teared up at everyone's comments. Wiping tears and waving her hands, she ordered everyone to get to work. "This quilt needs to be done so we can auction it off and make a lot of money for the children."

"So, Chandler, do you think Peter is going to buy the hardware store building?" Hillary asked after they'd been working a while.

"You know, I think he might," Chandler said, excited about the prospect. "He was talking about a partnership between Jake, Keith, Joshua, and himself. Keith and Joshua are both moving to town in the next month or so. They've even been talking about keeping the hardware theme going in the new place."

"How exciting!" Rosie exclaimed. "There's so much original architecture and fixtures in the place it would be a shame to get rid of it."

"And it would be in keeping with the rest of the storefronts in town," Fran added.

"Who would run the place?" Andrea asked. She didn't want them taking any of her staff.

"They mentioned something about Keith being interested because his dad used to own a bar and he helped out during college," Chandler explained. "Although I think we should refer to it as a tavern rather than a bar. That would be more in keeping with the history of our town. I know that my building was the original town tavern, but the hardware store is right next door, so it's fairly close to historically accurate."

"Maybe you could work there, Myrtle," Macy suggested, smiling. "Have any more hidden talents?" she asked sarcastically. The younger ladies were still in shock over the revelation that Myrtle had been a barmaid in her early years.

"You know, Macy, I may just look into that," Myrtle replied. And she was only half kidding. "I might be able to teach the younger generation a thing or two."

"I'd pay money to watch you work behind a bar again," Fran teased.

"And I'd charge you, too, Fran," Myrtle responded, to the delight of the rest of the ladies.

"Myrtle, I'd be more than happy to let the guys know they already have one employee," Chandler joked. She'd bet money that Myrtle was serious about this new career choice.

"Just make sure you tell them I don't do dishes," Myrtle declared, dead serious. "Don't want these beautiful hands to get all wrinkled," she insisted, holding up hands that were already wrinkled and arthritic, causing raucous laughter from the crowd.

"I'll keep that in mind," Chandler acknowledged, trying to keep a straight face.

"Alright ladies," Rosie said, looking at the clock, "it's nine-thirty, and I think it's also time to turn the quilt. You've managed to work and talk at the same time tonight. Myrtle, would you please do the honors?"

Mary Ann and Candy removed the stops at each end of the frame, and Myrtle spun the take-up pole to advance the quilt to the next section to be quilted. After straightening the layers, they returned the stops to their original position, keeping the quilt taut and stationary.

"All set for next week," Myrtle announced. "Hope we all have a great, uneventful week."

"Here, here!" Fran cheered with an imaginary toast.

Chapter 30

"I can't believe you're getting married tomorrow!" Macy cried as she walked into the bakery a few Fridays later. It had been a whirlwind couple of weeks leading up to Chandler and Peter's big day. Macy and Jake had spent more time together than apart, getting closer and closer each week.

When she was alone, there were times that Macy would allow herself to think of what it would be like if she and Jake were getting married. She had needed to remind herself that no one had mentioned anything about marriage.

"I know!" Chandler cried back, handing Macy a fresh cinnamon roll and a cup of hot coffee. Fall had arrived, and the hot coffee was just what she needed to take the chill off. It was the first weekend in November, after all, and the mornings were chilly. Fortunately, the afternoons were still in the seventies.

Chandler poured herself a cup and turned to face Macy. "Luann came home from college last night to help us get everything set in the bakery. I don't know if Gretchen and I could have gotten everything done without her."

"Well, I have today off, so I'm all yours," Macy told her. "What's first on the to-do list?"

"Oh my," Chandler sighed, plopping down on the chair across from Macy and looking over her notes. "Gretchen, Luann, and Andrea are taking care of all the food and beverages. They told me to trust them and not worry about a thing." Continuing down her list, "The garden club is handling all the flowers, and the Advice Quilting Bee is handling the decorations. Thanks to Peter's generous donations, the football team and fire department will be helping with set up and tear down tomorrow." She got to the bottom of the list. "Looks to me like all you and I have to do is look beautiful!"

"Wow, this is a community event," Macy said, amazed by the outpouring of help from the community. She thought it might be that the residents were willing to help because they were so grateful for all Peter had done to breathe new life into the town.

"The rehearsal is at five o'clock this evening, and then we'll go to the Hilltop for dinner. Peter and I felt it important to include as many of the businesses as we could. Since Andrea is catering the reception, it was only fair to have the rehearsal dinner there."

"What time are we meeting Nadine for our mani-pedis?" Macy asked, finishing up her cinnamon roll. There was only one nail salon within twenty miles of Hope Springs, in a neighboring town.

"Two o'clock," Chandler answered. "That should still give us plenty of time to come back and get ready for the rehearsal."

"And I confirmed that Mabel's daughter is bringing her crew from her salon in the city to my house tomorrow morning at nine for hair and makeup," Macy added. "Since the ceremony is at two-thirty, that should be good. Rosie and Myrtle are coming as well. I think Myrtle feels like your surrogate grandmother," she laughed.

"She kind of is," Chandler agreed, smiling. "After my grandmother passed away, Myrtle took over the job, even though by then I was in my twenties."

Chandler looked over her list one more time. "I think that's about it. Since you took the day off, let's go over to Hillary's and see if there's anything good in her Thursday consignment delivery. It's after ten, so she'll be open." She turned back to Gretchen, who'd been working behind the counter on a birthday cake due later in the day. "Luann should be in anytime now, but if you need anything, call me."

Gretchen stepped back from the cake. "Don't you worry about a thing. We've got everything under control. I don't want to see you back in here today or tomorrow. This is your weekend to pamper yourself. Enjoy every minute of it."

"Thank you so much for everything," Chandler said, tearing up a bit. "I don't know how I was lucky enough to find such wonderful employees and friends."

"Oh, get out of here before I start crying on this cake," Gretchen teased.

Macy and Chandler walked across the street just as Myrtle and Fran were coming out of the mercantile. It was a good thing they were both wearing sunglasses because the sun bouncing off Myrtle's lime green top was enough to blind a person.

"Good morning, girls," Fran greeted them. "We were just going to Hillary's to see if we might find something for my friend here to wear tomorrow," she explained, pointing to Myrtle. "Apparently, she forgot she has an important role, and I didn't think you'd want her wearing her spandex tights and knit top."

"Oh, stop," Myrtle admonished, "I knew I needed to get something but just never had the time to go shopping."

"Well, what have you been doing all this time?" Fran countered.

"Spying on all of us," Macy threw in. Seeing the shocked look on Myrtle's face, she cautioned, "Now, Myrtle, Jake and I have seen you and Mabel sneaking around in the evenings under the pretense of taking a walk to see if we're out on the porch. You know if you're going to do a recon mission, it might be wise not to wear something that glows in the dark."

"I don't know what you're talking about," Myrtle countered, with her nose in the air. "That was the best time of day when we could get our exercise." She fluffed her hair and pulled her top down tighter over her double-knit slacks.

"Uh, huh," Macy agreed, laughing. "Next time, why don't you say hi on your way by?"

"Okay, Myrtle, let's get you into Hillary's so we can see if there's something more appropriate for you to wear tomorrow," Chandler guided the group into the store.

Hillary excused herself from the two other customers shopping in the front of the store to greet the foursome and lead them back to the new merchandise.

As they looked through the racks for something appropriate for Myrtle, Macy happened upon a dress she wanted to try on. "I'm heading to the dressing room, ladies," she told them.

"I'm right behind you," Chandler told her, "I want to try this on as well." She held up a pantsuit she thought would be suitable for her honeymoon.

As Macy was in the process of putting on the dress she had chosen, she could hear the ladies in the front talking. They must have been right next to her dressing room.

"I heard he's dating his nurse," one woman whispered, loud enough for Macy to hear.

"And get this," the other one said, "My sister knew this nurse from the practice she went to in the city. Apparently, she was having an affair with the doctor there. Nearly broke up his marriage."

"How could Dr. Grainger possibly want to be with someone like that?!" the first one sneered. "I think my Patricia would be so much better for him. I think I'll invite him to dinner so I can introduce them."

Macy just wanted to melt into the floor. What was it about this dressing room that every time she was in it, the customers were talking about her?! She was about to step out and say something when she heard a familiar voice.

"You two ought to be ashamed of yourselves. What gives you the right to judge someone without having even met them? Do you even know her name? My guess is no, you don't! I'm sure if I started digging, I could find out dirt about each one of you. And trust me, when your husbands were younger, they weren't angels. So, if I were you, I'd put a lid on it and keep your nasty opinions and gossip to yourselves."

Macy wasn't sure what happened next because she was still in the dressing room, but apparently, the pair didn't appreciate the tongue lashing they had just received. She thought she heard one of them say something to Hillary about needing to leave, and then she heard the bell over the front door jingle. Macy stepped out of the dressing room to find all her friends cautiously looking at her. She stood in front of the three-way mirror. "Well, what do you think?" she asked them.

"Are you okay, sweetie?" Hillary dared to ask, knowing Macy had heard every word.

"Of course, I have the best support system in the world," Macy told them all. "And now you all know that I had an affair with a married man."

"Sweetheart, we knew that months ago," Fran told Macy, giving her a side hug.

"How did you find out?" Macy knew that Chandler wouldn't tell anyone.

"Same way those two heard," Myrtle explained. "From someone who knew someone who was a patient there. But unlike those two, we also knew that he was using you to get back at his wife and partner. We think what he did was wrong and don't think any less of you for it, so don't even put that thought in your head."

How did Macy get so lucky in the friend department? "But Myrtle, do you really have dirt on their husbands?" she asked, curious.

"You bet I do, honey. The perks of being a barmaid," Myrtle winked. "Now, I need to try this on and see if it passes muster." She held up a very sedate evergreen shift dress and matching beaded jacket.

Myrtle came out a few minutes later to stand in front of the mirror. "Oh, Myrtle," Chandler gushed, coming to stand behind her. "You look stunning."

Myrtle looked in the mirror and almost didn't recognize herself. With a tear in her eye, she whispered, "I clean up pretty well, don't I?"

"Yes, you do, and I'm so proud you're representing my side of the family tomorrow," Chandler said as she hugged her.

"Okay, ladies," Hillary interrupted, "let's get this sale moving before you cry all over my clothes!"

After another successful shopping trip to Hillary's, they decided they'd better stop in at the diner for some lunch before their nail appointment. Fran needed to get back to her store, but Myrtle said she'd join them.

Peter and Jake were having lunch there, so they pushed another table up to all sit together. After ordering drinks and lunch, they talked about how all the plans were going. Peter assured Chandler that everything was under control and didn't want her to worry about anything. "Really, honey, just relax," he insisted.

Chandler was just about to say something when they were interrupted by the pair that had been at Hillary's. "Dr. Grainger!" the one whose daughter was named Patricia exclaimed. "I'd love to invite you to have dinner at our home one evening next week," she insisted. "That's what we do in small towns—invite the new doctor for dinner."

Jake looked a bit taken aback. "Oh, thank you for the invitation. Would you mind calling the medical center and leaving your information with Suzie? I'm not sure what my schedule is for next week."

"Sure, I'll do that this afternoon," she told him, and then as she shot Myrtle an obnoxious look, she added, "Looking forward to having you in our home, Doctor."

After the pair had walked away, Jake said, "That's the first dinner invitation I've received. Should I be expecting more of them?"

"Let's hope not," Macy sneered. "Are you really going to go?"

"Probably," he answered, "I'd hate for word to get around that the new doctor is a snob."

"Just be careful," Myrtle cautioned. "Remember what happened at the Labor Day celebration?" referring to the grandmothers throwing their granddaughters at him. "I won't be there to run interference this time."

"Warning duly noted," Jake told her.

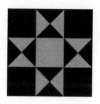

Chapter 31

Saturday morning was a flurry of activity at Macy's house. Chandler had arrived with pastries from the bakery, Rosie and Myrtle came ready to be pampered with hair and makeup, and by two in the afternoon, they were all ready to go. Since the weather was a balmy seventy degrees and sunny, they decided to walk to the visitor's center, where they would hide out until it was time to start the ceremony. Chandler didn't want anyone seeing her before then.

At precisely two-twenty, once most of the guests were seated, which included quite a bit of the town, Rosie and Myrtle walked over to the park and found their seats in front. Peter's father, James, and his fiancé Victoria were seated next to Rosie. Peter was so thankful he'd decided family was more important than anything and made up with his father just before he proposed to Chandler. Robert, Mary Ann, and their daughter, Missy, sat behind them.

At two-thirty, the string quartet began playing the wedding music. Peter and Jake stood at the altar, or in this case, the top steps of the gazebo, with the minister.

Macy slowly walked up the aisle. If she hadn't been wearing her merlot bridesmaid dress, one would think she was the bride because of the huge smile she wore. Once she got to the first row of chairs, she stepped to the left and turned around. She stole a glance at Jake and saw that he was looking at her and smiling as well.

The music changed, announcing that the bride was next. Everyone stood and turned toward the back. Chandler came up the aisle smiling at everyone along the way and came to stand next to Peter.

And thus began the ceremony. Within fifteen minutes, they were pronounced man and wife, with cheers from the crowd. As they turned and faced everyone, Chandler saw that most of the residents of Hope Springs was in attendance. They'd invited anyone who had helped with their special day. That included the ladies of the garden club, the football team and their parents, and the members of the volunteer fire department who helped with the reception set up.

Peter decided they'd better address their guests. "Chandler and I would like to thank all of you for helping to make our day so special. In our eyes, you are all our family, and we are so grateful for all you've done. Please join us for the reception here in the park."

Everyone filed out and meandered their way around toward the huge reception tent the fire department had erected in case of inclement weather. The family had been asked to stay behind for pictures, including Myrtle. Once they finished, they made their way over to the reception tent.

While Macy and Jake were waiting for the last few shots involving them, he whispered in her ear, "You look beautiful." Seeing her blush and give him a shy smile, he continued, "I was actually envisioning that being us instead of Peter and Chandler."

Before she could respond, the photographer was calling for them. Macy couldn't remember the rest of the photo shoot. All she thought about was what Jake had whispered in her ear. As much as she wanted to believe he wanted to marry her, she was still hesitant to think something so wonderful could happen to her.

Jake pulled her from her thoughts to lead her to the reception tent, where they were swallowed up by people talking about everything from what a beautiful ceremony it was to what a great couple Chandler and Peter made.

Soon the bride and groom made their entrance into the reception, and everyone enjoyed an evening of good food, drink, and dancing, with music provided by a local high school student who owned his own disc jockey business. Peter and Chandler did want to make their wedding a community event.

Macy thought she'd never danced more in her life. She learned many line dances from the high school kids in attendance but loved moving to the slow songs with Jake. It reminded her of the first time they danced together in this very park on Labor Day. Just being in his arms evoked all kinds of emotions and thoughts of a future together.

Off to the side, the Little Old Lady Network was watching the show on the dance floor. "It won't be long before we have another wedding," Myrtle told them.

Fran shook her head. "I hate to agree with you, Myrtle, but it definitely seems you were right about Macy and Jake. It's amazing how fast love grows in Hope Springs."

"I agree," said Mabel, who hardly ever said anything. "They've been together almost every evening, from what I can tell." Since she lived right next door to Jake, she had a better view than any of the others.

Myrtle continued her perusal of the reception space. Her eyes caught sight of another couple near the food tables.

"Looks like we may have another couple on our hands," she informed the group.

"Who might that be?" Fran asked, trying to see which direction Myrtle was looking.

"Over by the food tables," Myrtle said. "Looks like Peter's friend Keith may have eyes for Andrea."

Fran looked to see what Myrtle saw. "Oh, good heavens, they're just talking! He's probably asking her what the specials are at the diner since he's moving to town."

"I'm thinking he's hoping Andrea is the special," Myrtle chuckled. "We'll just have to keep an eye on things and see how it progresses."

"I don't know, Myrtle. I think one relationship at a time is more than we can handle," Mabel protested. "We don't even have Jake and Macy engaged yet."

"I wouldn't be surprised if Macy and Jake were engaged by the end of the night," Myrtle stated.

Fran loved Myrtle's romantic enthusiasm, but not her insistence that they help every couple in Hope Springs find happiness. "Myrtle, let's just give it a rest for a while."

"What are we discussing over here?" Rosie asked, interrupting the conversation.

Myrtle knew Rosie wouldn't like what they were planning, so she dodged the question. "Don't Chandler and Peter look so happy?"

Rosie had known Myrtle long enough to know that Chandler and Peter's happiness wasn't what the group was discussing. Most likely, they were talking about Macy and

Jake and what they could do to help seal the deal. "Yes, they do, and so do Macy and Jake."

"Yes, I suppose they do as well," Myrtle agreed, trying to show disinterest in the latter couple.

She didn't fool Rosie. "Oh, Myrtle, please tell me you aren't going to interfere in another relationship."

Myrtle put her hand to her chest. "Me? What makes you think I would ever interfere in anyone's relationship?"

Rosie and the others leaned back away from Myrtle.

"What are you all doing?" Myrtle demanded.

"Waiting for the lightning to strike you," Fran told her. Myrtle slapped her on the arm, and everyone else started laughing. "Come on, Myrtle, let's go dance," Fran ordered as the music sped up.

Chandler and Peter stood looking at all their guests having such a good time. If they wanted it to be a community party, they succeeded. The party continued well into the night, as no one was in a hurry to go home.

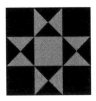

Chapter 32

"Now, don't forget you're having dinner at the Clifford's tonight, Dr. Grainger," Suzie informed Jake when he walked into the medical center the following Friday morning. True to her word, Mrs. Clifford called Suzie the previous Friday afternoon to schedule the dinner. At first, he wasn't sure who Suzie had been referring to, but then he remembered the conversation in the diner and put two and two together. Since Mrs. Clifford had not introduced herself by name, he had no idea who she was.

"What time is that?" he asked. He didn't want to be late, or early for that matter.

"Six-thirty," Suzie informed him. "Don't be late."

The medical center was unusually busy, mostly with flu shots and those suffering from ear infections and allergies. By closing time, Jake was beat. All he wanted to do was spend his evening with Macy, but unfortunately, he had dinner with the Cliffords on his schedule. "I'd rather be spending my evening with you," he whined to Macy when he came into the exam room she was restocking. He came up behind her and wrapped his arms around her. "Can't I just call and tell them I'm sick or something?"

Macy smiled, loving the feeling of being held so gently. "As much as I'd like to tell you to do that, I can't." She turned to face him, wrapping her arms around his waist.

"You need to stop whining and put your big boy pants on and go to dinner at the Clifford's. Just know that if you see my light on, you can always stop by later for a glass of wine." She kissed him on the cheek.

"Oh, alright, I'll stop whining," he said, smiling before he gently kissed her on the lips. "Dinner is at six-thirty, so maybe I'll be at your house by seven-thirty."

Macy leaned back to look up at him with a questioning look. "Only one hour, really?"

"I'll say I'm too full for dessert," he cooed, snuggling into her neck. "I'll get that at your house."

Macy sighed. "As wonderful as that sounds, I think you'd better stay for dessert if offered."

"Okay," he said reluctantly. He kissed her soundly again. "I'll see you at eight-thirty," he added as he walked out of the room.

Macy just shook her head and went back to restocking the shelves.

By closing time, Macy was exhausted but excited at the prospect of seeing Jake after his dinner at the Cliffords. Myrtle had told her that Mrs. Clifford was ready to steal Jake away from Macy for her daughter, Patricia. *Over my dead body!* she thought.

Macy walked up her sidewalk just as the mailman was walking down. She thanked him for delivering her mail and continued up the steps. She opened the flap on her mailbox attached to the wall by the front door. Macy had always wanted to live in a house that had the mailbox attached. She thought it was so quaint and small-town. As she took the mail out, a large envelope dropped, face-up, on the floor of the front porch. As Macy bent to pick it up, she looked at the return address and fell to her knees.

Oh, my goodness! Macy inwardly screamed, shaking as she picked up the envelope. She looked around to see if anyone had noticed her on her knees. Quickly getting up, Macy hurriedly unlocked her door and raced inside. She ran to the kitchen and dropped everything, including the envelope, on the table. Grabbing a glass from the cabinet, she filled it with cold water from the automatic dispenser on her refrigerator. She downed the glass and filled it again, all the while staring at the large envelope on the table. *Why now? After all these years, why now?*

Macy didn't recognize the handwriting, but she knew who'd sent it. "Just when I've gotten my life in order, now you reach out to me!" she yelled at the envelope. "I have a good life here, and I don't need for you to be messing it up!" She practically slammed her glass on the table in protest. Then she sat down and burst into uncontrollable sobs.

Macy wasn't sure how long she'd been sitting at the table when a persistent banging brought her back to reality. Realizing someone was knocking on her door, she wiped her tears and walked to the front door to see who the visitor was. She opened the door and practically fell into Rosie's arms.

Chapter 33

Rosie had been feeling all day that one of her Advice Quilting Bee members was in distress. She'd seen many of the members throughout the day at the shop and all seemed well. But the feeling just kept getting stronger the closer it got to closing time.

"Mary Ann, I'm going to head out," Rosie informed her daughter-in-law as she headed toward the door. "It's a nice evening, so I think I'll walk over to see if Macy is home." For some reason, the young woman was on her mind.

"No problem, Candy and I can handle things," Mary Ann assured her.

Rosie took the short walk to Macy's and knocked on the front door. Through the small side window, she could see that Macy was sitting in the kitchen and appeared to be crying. *This is where I'm supposed to be,* she thought. She banged louder. She finally saw Macy look up and come to the door, wiping her tears along the way.

Macy flung open the door, practically throwing herself into Rosie's arms. Oh, it felt good. *This must be what it feels like to be hugged by your mom,* Macy thought. Even though she didn't want to let go, it was cool, and she didn't want Rosie catching a chill. Macy stepped back and motioned for Rosie to enter, closing the door behind her.

Macy wiped the tears from her cheeks. "I'm so sorry I practically attacked you, Rosie. I'm not usually like that. Can I get you something to drink?"

Rosie smiled. "My dear, you have nothing to apologize for. I was sent here to check on you, and clearly, there was a reason."

Macy looked at her quizzically. "Who sent you? No one knows about it." Macy walked back to the kitchen to get Rosie a glass of water.

Taking the glass from the young woman, Rosie took a drink and said, "I have been having a feeling all day that one of my friends needed comfort. As I was getting ready to leave the shop, your face popped into my head. So, I decided to come by to check on you."

Macy motioned for Rosie to have a seat at the kitchen table. "I'm not sure what to make of that, but you're right. I was definitely in need of a hug when you showed up."

"What has you so upset, child?" Rosie asked with compassion in her voice.

Macy figured if she could trust anyone, it would be Rosie. She took a deep breath. "Okay, here goes. Remember when I told you my parents weren't the greatest parents in the world?" Once Rosie acknowledged the question, Macy went on to explain all about the foster homes and how she'd realized early on that she had to care for herself. She took a drink of water, feeling dehydrated, but was also trying to gauge Rosie's reaction. Since she didn't see a shocked expression on Rosie's face, she decided to continue.

"Once I was eighteen, I was on my own. I got a job in a restaurant and managed to find a room to rent I could afford. And I enrolled in nursing school. I was determined not to end up like my parents. I graduated with honors, immediately went to work, and you know the rest of the story."

"Yes, but I don't think that is why I felt the urge to come here today." Rosie knew there had to be more to the story, and the only way for Macy to move on was to let go of the past.

Macy took another deep breath. "Well, as I said before, my dad went to prison when I was six for dealing drugs. Unfortunately, he got in a jail fight and was killed." She stopped for a minute. "You know, when I learned about it years later, I really didn't care. He wasn't a very nice man," she said, with a sad smile.

"And your mom?" Rosie asked. She had a feeling this was where the root of the problem was.

"My mom," Macy sighed with a tearful smile. "Well, last I heard, she was living in the city in a halfway house. She came to see me after I got my first job, asking for money. She said she'd read in the paper that I'd graduated and figured out where I lived. I told her I wasn't going to give her anything because she'd just use it to buy more drugs. She got mad, said some nasty things, and left. I know that may seem cold and heartless, Rosie, but I was just beginning to have my head above water, and I was trying to make it on my own. I didn't want my mom to suck me dry," Macy began crying again.

Rosie got up and went to the bathroom in search of tissues. She looked up toward the ceiling and prayed that God would give her the words needed to comfort Macy. *Lord, this child has been through so much. You've given her the strength to get through it so far. I hope you will continue to be a presence in her life because I have the feeling there is more yet to come.*

Rosie made her way back to the kitchen and handed the tissues to a still crying Macy. "Okay, let's dry your tears and see if we can make sense of all this."

Macy took the tissues from Rosie and wiped her tears, blowing her nose as well. She gave out a little laugh. "Bet you weren't expecting to walk in on this today, were you?"

"The Lord puts me where I need to be," Rosie assured her, "and today it's here with you. Now, let's talk about this envelope because I'm guessing this is the cause of all your tears." Rosie pointed to the envelope on the table. "Am I right?"

Macy looked again at the envelope that started her crying fit. "It's from my mom."

"I see. Do you want me to leave so you can open it?" Rosie would understand if she wanted to be alone.

Macy shook her head. "No, would you mind staying?" Seeing Rosie smile, Macy picked up the envelope. Her hands started shaking. "Would you mind opening it?" she asked, handing the large envelope to Rosie.

Rosie carefully opened the envelope and took out a letter. Along with the letter was a pink envelope addressed to Macy. But the postmaster had marked "Return to Sender" across the address. Rosie looked at the date. It had been postmarked two years earlier. Before reading the letter, she looked at the large outer envelope. "Macy, someone mailed this letter last week, but the pink envelope postmark was dated two years ago."

Macy looked at the contents of the large envelope. Sure enough, the pink envelope had her mom's handwriting, but the letter accompanying it wasn't from her mom. As she began trying to read the letter, her hands shook so much she couldn't hold the paper still. She asked Rosie if she would mind reading it to her out loud.

"Dear Miss Greenburg, It is with sadness that we must inform you that your mother, Patsy Greenburg, passed away on July 25th. We had a difficult time finding you but were glad we were finally able to locate you through your current employer, Dr. Grainger. He was kind enough to give us your home address." The letter explained where her mother was buried, right next to her father, in plots Macy's grandfather had left for them. As Rosie read through the rest of the letter, all Macy could focus on was the fact that Jake knew that her mother had passed and never told her a thing. Why? She'd told him everything when she'd had the flu. Why didn't he tell her about her mother being deceased!?

"Macy, honey, did you know Jake knew about your mother?" Rosie asked as she set the letter on the table.

"No!" Macy cried. "He's never said a thing! Why wouldn't he say anything? I don't understand!" She felt so betrayed.

"There must be some good explanation as to why he never told you," Rosie said, hoping she was right. There had to be something they were missing. She thought maybe they had talked to Suzie, the office administrator, but the letter clearly stated "Dr. Grainger". "Would you like for me to talk to him to see if I can find out what's going on?" Rosie asked Macy.

Macy wiped more tears from her eyes, "No, this is my problem, Rosie. I think I should be the one to talk to him." She looked at the letter again and realized that her parents were buried in the next town, only about twenty minutes away. "Rosie, when I'm ready, would you mind going with me to visit my parents? They aren't too far from here."

Rosie covered Macy's hand with hers. "I'd be happy to. Just tell me when and I'll be ready."

"Thank you," Macy whispered. She looked down at the table at the pink envelope with her name on it. "I don't think I'm quite ready to open this yet."

Rosie understood; the child had been through enough. Who knew what her mother had written, given their final conversation? "You'll know when the time is right," she advised. Rosie looked up at the clock and saw that it was almost eight. "I hate to leave you like this, but I really should be making my way home."

"Of course, would you like for me to walk you home?" Macy asked as they stood up from the table and walked toward the front door.

"No, dear, I'll be fine. The street lights are on." As Macy opened the front door, Rosie gave her a big hug. "I'll keep you in my prayers. But please, before you jump to conclusions, ask Jake what happened. Maybe he didn't know."

"I will. Thank you for being here for me." Macy hugged her again. Once Rosie was down the steps and on her way, Macy walked back into her house and closed the door. She could see the pink envelope on the kitchen table but had no desire to open it. The interesting thing was that she was more devastated by the possibility that Jake had lied than the realization that her mother was gone. She sat on the sofa and turned on the television, hoping there would be something to take her mind off everything.

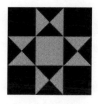

Chapter 34

Jake thought dinner would never end. Mrs. Clifford was probably the worst cook in all of Virginia. He wasn't even sure what he'd eaten, and he would probably need the castor oil he'd prescribed to Myrtle and her friends before the night was out. Mr. Clifford was more interested in the ballgame on television than visiting with his guest, and Patricia's voice was giving him a headache. All he could think about was getting to Macy as fast as he could.

The only bright spot of the whole evening was when he looked out the front window and saw Myrtle and other members of the network behind the hedges with binoculars trying to get a look inside.

Fortunately, a little after eight, just before dessert was to be served, he received a text from Rosie. It was something about Macy needing him ASAP. "I'm so sorry, Mrs. Clifford, but I'm afraid one of my patients needs me," Jake tried sounding apologetic.

Mrs. Clifford was the only one in the room who looked disappointed that he was leaving before dessert. "You really have to go?"

"I'm afraid so. That's what happens when you're the only doctor in town. You're always on call," he explained as he made his way toward the door. "Thank you for a lovely evening," he said to be polite. He turned to her husband, who wasn't listening to a word Jake said. "Don't get up. I can see myself out."

It wasn't until he was hurrying down the sidewalk that he realized he hadn't said anything to Patricia. Oh well, that should take care of any future relationship.

Jake didn't question why Rosie was texting for Macy; he just wanted to get to her quickly. He passed Myrtle and her posse on his way and told them he hoped they enjoyed the show. He heard Myrtle try to deny it and Fran ask her to shut up, but he kept walking.

When he got to Macy's, he could see that she was on the couch watching television in the front window. She didn't appear to be in distress. He knocked on the door.

Macy turned and saw Jake standing at her front door. *Darn it!* she thought to herself. *I forgot he was stopping by if he saw the lights on.* She reached for the remote and turned off the television before walking to the door and opening it.

"How was your dinner?" Macy asked in a quiet voice.

Jake could tell something had changed. He looked at her carefully, trying to figure it out. "Um, well, Mrs. Clifford is a horrible cook. I may need some castor oil later." He waited to see if she remembered their first day working together but got no response. He bent down to kiss her, and Macy turned away and walked toward the kitchen.

Jake followed, not sure what to make of her demeanor. "Is everything okay?" he asked, tentatively.

Macy picked the letter up off the table and handed it to him. "Read this," she ordered.

As Jake scanned the letter, he realized why she was acting so strangely. "Macy, honey, I'm so sorry about your mom," he consoled, trying to hug her.

"That's all you've got to say? Did you read the entire letter?" She couldn't believe he didn't deny the words on the page.

"Yes, I read the entire letter," he answered, not sure why she was upset with him. "Am I missing something here? I didn't kill your mother."

Macy couldn't believe him! "Not the part about my mother dying! I'm talking about the part where they called my current employer, Dr. Grainger, and he gave them my home address! You knew about this and never told me!" The tears began again. But this time for their relationship, which she knew was over.

Jake was wracking his brain to remember any conversation he'd had with a halfway house, and he couldn't remember any. "Macy, I honestly don't remember ever having that conversation. Don't you think that if I'd known any of this, I would have told you?" he pleaded.

"I don't know what to think, Jake!" Her voice was getting shriller with each word.

"Macy?" Jake didn't like where this was headed.

"I think I need to be alone," she whispered. "I just don't understand how you could keep something like this from me."

Jake put the letter back on the table next to the pink envelope. "For what it's worth, I don't remember talking to them," he said, pointing to the letter. "But I can see right now that doesn't seem to matter. So, I'll go and leave you alone. When you're ready to talk about all this," he said, waving his hand over the contents on the table, "I'll be around."

Jake turned and walked to the front door, with Macy following behind.

"I'm sorry," Jake whispered, sad for the little girl who had lost her parents. "I'm sorry you lost your parents. I'm sorry you had to raise yourself. But mostly, I'm sorry for all you've lost in your life, Macy. I hoped I'd be the guy who could give you the wonderful life you truly deserve. But I guess I was wrong."

Macy gave him a tear-filled smile. "I'm a product of the bad side of the foster care system. Maybe it's low self-esteem or something, but I was just kidding myself to think that I deserve the wonderful life you're talking about." The shame that she thought had long since disappeared reemerged with a vengeance. Whatever made her think she could have someone as wonderful as Jake? Here was the man of her dreams, and she didn't deserve him. She'd been told her whole life she wasn't good enough, and unfortunately, she believed it. She wasn't fortunate to have found a loving family to call her own as so many others had. No, she was always given to families who only wanted her for the money they got from the state.

"I'm not good enough for you, Jake. You deserve someone who doesn't have all my baggage. Someone social services isn't calling trying to find. I'm sorry I put you in that position."

"So, this is it?" Jake asked, not believing what he was hearing.

Macy tried to smile through her tears. "Yes, I think it is. Goodbye, Jake." Then she closed the door.

Jake stood there staring at the closed door. *What just happened?!* he thought. *One minute we're talking about her parents being dead, and the next she's breaking up with me?* He knew in the state Macy was in that it would be best if he just left and went home. Maybe he could see if he could get her to talk over the weekend before they had to see each other again on Monday at the medical center. In the meantime, he was going to try to find out who this halfway house talked to because it certainly hadn't been him.

Macy stood on the other side of the closed door, half wanting Jake to knock on the door and half wanting him to go away. When she heard his footsteps going off the porch, Macy slid to the floor in a puddle of tears.

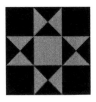

Chapter 35

Macy had slept horribly. She kept playing the events of the previous night in her mind. Getting the letter from the halfway house, seeing her mother's handwriting, and finding out that she had died was bad enough. But the realization that Jake had known and hadn't told her was too much. The funny thing was that she had told him she was breaking up with him because she wasn't good enough for him. *Was I using his lying as the excuse because I knew he wouldn't buy the fact that I felt inferior?* Macy wasn't sure. She just knew that at that very moment, she was having a hard time forgiving him for not letting her know her mother had passed.

Macy got out of bed and went into the kitchen for some much-needed coffee. The pink envelope stared at her almost, willing her to open it, but Macy wasn't ready for that yet. She walked past it to the cabinet to get the coffee can down to make a pot. It was then that she remembered she'd used the rest the previous morning. "Crap," she groaned. "Guess I'll get dressed and go to the diner for breakfast." She hoped Jake wouldn't be there. She wasn't ready to see him yet. She went to her bedroom to throw on some sweats and put her hair in a ponytail. She didn't even have the will or energy to shower.

Walking into the diner a short time later, Macy saw that Myrtle, Fran, and Mabel were seated in a booth along the wall. While she wanted to eat alone, Macy wasn't sure how to bypass them, especially when Myrtle was waving at her like a crazy person. Fortunately, none of them knew what had transpired, so she would just try to act like everything was normal.

"Hi, ladies," Macy greeted them, hoping she sounded happier than she felt.

Alicia came over and poured her a cup of coffee. "Hi, Macy. Jake was in here earlier. Said he was heading to the city for the day," Alicia informed her. "Thought you'd be going along."

Guess Jake wasn't as distraught as I thought he'd be, Macy thought, stirring her coffee. "Oh, I had things to do today, so he went without me," not really telling a lie. She did have things to do at home, and he did go without her.

"Okay, ladies, do you know what you'd like for breakfast?" Alicia asked the table.

The others all ordered plates laden with eggs, sausage, hash browns, and sides of toast. Macy's stomach just wasn't up for that much food, so she just ordered a short stack of hotcakes and a bowl of fruit.

"I'll put that order in for you ladies," Alicia told them, taking their menus and putting them under her arm before walking back to the kitchen.

"Chandler and Peter should be coming home today, right?" Mabel asked.

Macy smiled. "Yes, sometime this evening." Oh, how she'd missed her best friend. "I think they're planning on living at Chandler's, at least for now."

Fran noticed that Macy didn't quite seem herself. "Is everything okay, honey?"

Leave it to Fran to be the observant one in the group, Macy thought. "Yes, just a little tired this morning," Macy insisted. "Probably from having to walk up here without coffee."

"None at your house, huh?" Myrtle asked. Macy hoped Myrtle wouldn't pry.

Macy chuckled. "Apparently, it's been a while since I've made a grocery run. Fran, do you have any ground coffee in the can at the mercantile?"

"Sure do," Fran assured her. "I know that not everyone owns those fancy one cup at a time coffeemakers."

"I'll stop by on my way home to get some," Macy said.

Alicia delivered their breakfasts, and Macy listened to her friends reminisce about what life had been like in Hope Springs back in the day. The hotcakes she'd ordered were beginning to weigh heavy in her stomach, but the fruit helped to keep them down. She was surprised she'd been able to eat anything, given the current state of her nerves.

After breakfast, Macy went to Rosie's Quilting Emporium. She had no particular reason to go, except she was sure Rosie would want to know how she was, and Macy just didn't want to go home.

"Hi, Mary Ann," Macy said as she entered the store. "Is Rosie around?"

"Hi, Macy!" Mary Ann was always so cheerful. Macy figured the woman had never had a bad day in her life. "Yes, she is. I think she's back by the quilting frame if

233

you'd like to go see her." She motioned for Macy to go toward the back of the store.

"Thanks," Macy said, walking to the back of the store.

Rosie was indeed sitting at the quilting frame, working on a section of the Christmas quilt. "Come and sit with me, Macy," Rosie insisted, never looking up from her stitching.

"Okay," Macy did as she was told. She automatically went to her section of the quilt and began working.

"I like to come back here and work when the store is quiet," Rosie explained. "It's very relaxing."

Macy smiled at the last comment because sometimes she was so worried about making every stitch perfect that she was a nervous wreck.

As if reading Macy's mind, Rosie asked, "Macy, have you ever seen a quilt made by the Amish?"

"No, I don't believe I have," Macy answered, wondering where Rosie was going with this.

"When the Amish make a quilt, they always make sure there is at least one mistake somewhere in the quilt. Do you know why?" Rosie continued stitching, not looking up at Macy.

Macy thought about it for a minute, "No, I don't think I do." She also continued stitching.

Rosie stopped and put down her needle. She looked up at Macy. "Because only God is perfect."

Macy stopped what she was doing and looked up at Rosie.

"Macy, we all make mistakes. None of us are perfect," Rosie told her. "Now, I'm guessing by the sad look in your eyes which matches the look I saw in Jake's eyes earlier this morning, that things didn't go well last night."

"Rosie, how do you know Jake was at my house last night? Did Myrtle have her spies out?!" Macy hoped that wasn't the case. They hadn't said anything at breakfast.

"No, child, it wasn't Myrtle. I sent Jake to you." Seeing Macy's confused look, Rosie continued. "When I left, you were so distraught. I'd hoped that by sending him to you, you would be able to clear everything up. But I'm guessing I was wrong."

Macy gave a sad little laugh. "We cleared it up alright. Jake knew everything and didn't tell me."

"He told you that?" Rosie calmly asked.

Macy shook her head, "No, he denied it. But I didn't believe him, Rosie. He told me he hadn't spoken to anyone, but there was no other explanation!"

Rosie picked up her needle and went back to stitching. "So that's it? Relationship over?"

Macy's shoulders slumped. "Yes, it's over. And now I have to go to work on Monday and pretend I never loved him." Macy wasn't sure how she was going to make that work, but she had to. She'd already left one job because of her feelings for the doctor, and she wasn't going to leave another.

"You are good enough for Jake if that's what you're thinking," Rosie quietly said. "We can keep telling you that, but you have to believe it yourself. Yes, you've been

235

through more than most of us, but you can't use this one event as the catalyst to push away the best thing that's happened to you. If this hadn't happened, you have to ask yourself if you still want to end the relationship. Telling him, you are a product of the foster care system and, therefore, not good enough for him isn't fair to Jake. Let him be the one to make that decision."

Macy knew Rosie was quoting her very words to Jake from the previous night as the final excuse for them breaking up. She was so confused. Macy got up from the quilt frame and hugged Rosie before leaving the store. She stopped by the mercantile to get her coffee and then headed home to lick her wounds.

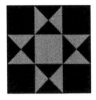

Chapter 36

As Jake drove to the halfway house following the GPS directions, he kept going over everything that had happened at Macy's. None of it made any sense. He couldn't understand why she didn't believe him. And then to keep saying she wasn't good enough for him. It was almost like she was looking for a reason to break things off.

Before he headed out of town, he'd seen Rosie and told her what Macy's excuses had been since she'd been the one to text him. She was the only other person in town who knew about the letter and Macy's mother. When he told her that Macy had said she wasn't good enough for him, Rosie, again, told him to be patient. He wasn't sure how much more patience he had left in him, but he truly loved Macy and wanted things to work.

Pulling up to the halfway house, Jake was flooded with memories of his residency. He thought he'd recognized the address when he'd seen the letter, but this confirmed it. He'd been to this very place several times to treat the sick residents. He briefly wondered if he'd ever encountered Macy's mother.

He walked in the front door and over to the small reception desk. The place was just as he'd remembered. Even though a housekeeping crew tried to keep it clean, there was a certain stench that was hard to forget.

A young woman, not more than twenty, looked up from an old computer. "May I help you?" she asked. Jake figured she might have been working there as part of her community service, as others had in the past.

"Yes, my name is Dr. Jake Grainger," he began before she interrupted.

"We didn't call for no doctor," she spat. Then she leaned back in her chair and yelled, "Hey Marge! Did someone call for a doctor?"

Jake looked past the girl to the doorway beyond where a woman emerged wearing a t-shirt with tropical flowers over skin-tight jeans and red spiked heels. Her hair was done up in a bouffant style reminiscent of the fifties. "No," Marge answered, in between chewing gum bites. "What'd you say your name was?"

"Dr. Jake Grainger," he repeated, "And this isn't a house call. I'm here because someone I know received a letter from this address telling her that her mom passed away and I need to talk to the person who wrote it. My friend's name is Macy Greenburg."

Jake watched as Marge's demeanor changed to one of all business. "Come with me," she ordered, waving for him to follow her to a back room.

They entered a room that looked to be someone's office, but one wall housed a floor-to-ceiling shelving unit full of cardboard boxes with names on them. "I was the one who wrote the letter. We've been trying to find Ms. Greenburg since her mother passed away. We finally caught a break when we found out she worked for you, and we called your office. I take it she received our letter?"

"Yes, she did, but to be honest, I don't remember talking to someone from here. Nor do I remember giving them Macy's home address," Jake informed her.

Marge walked behind the desk and sat down, reaching into a drawer, pulling out a file. "We make notes of everyone we speak to about a client, Dr. Grainger," Marge said as she opened the file. She put on reading glasses that had been dangling from a chain around her neck, similar to the ones he'd seen Myrtle and Fran wear. "It says here that we spoke to someone named Suzie. I take it she works for you?" she asked, looking over her glasses at Jake.

"Yes, she does," Jake answered, sitting down in the empty chair across the desk. "Did your people tell Suzie about Macy's mother passing away?" He thought that if she knew, surely Suzie would have told Macy.

"No, we don't divulge personal information over the phone," Marge assured him. "We would have just said we had something to mail to Ms. Greenburg and asked for a current home address. For privacy reasons, we wouldn't send mail to an employer's address."

"I see." Jake could understand the confidentiality issues. "But when the letter was typed, it stated that the person had talked to me, making Macy think that I was the one who gave the information and that I knew about her mother." He knew that Marge had no idea the trouble that had caused, but he had to understand why they did it that way.

"Oh, well, you met our clerical help out front, Dr. Grainger. Not exactly head of the class in secretarial school. I guess that she saw your name and took it from there."

Marge got up and walked over to the wall of boxes. She took one from the third shelf, marked Patsy Greenburg, and placed it on the desk. "These are Patsy's personal effects.

As we do with every resident who passes without next of kin present, we took them from her room and placed them in this box. I figured once we heard back from Ms. Greenburg, we'd make sure she got them." She slid the box across the desk. "Would you like to take them to her?"

Jake looked at the file box and thought how sad it was that this was all that was left of Macy's mother. "Yes, I can do that. Would you mind if I looked at the contents before leaving?"

"Help yourself. I'm going to head out, but you can stay as long as you need," Marge said, heading toward the door.

"One more question," Jake turned to her. "Why was the pink envelope included in the letter instead of just leaving it in the box?"

"About a month before Patsy died, she showed me the pink envelope and explained that she'd tried to mail it to Macy once, but it came back undeliverable. I guess Macy must have moved to Hope Springs by then. Anyway, she asked that if she passed while she was still living here, would I please make sure Macy got the letter before she got the rest of this stuff." Marge pointed to the box on the desk. "I don't know what is in the pink envelope, but it was very important to Patsy that I follow her request, so I put it in the notification letter."

"Thank you," Jake said with a smile. "You have been most helpful."

Before turning to leave, she added, "You could tell Patsy loved Macy and hated that she couldn't be the mother Macy needed her to be. For what it's worth, she was very proud of Macy."

After Marge left, Jake turned and stared at the box before him. He opened the lid and was quite shocked by what he saw. Inside were photos of Macy as a baby up until she was taken away from her parents. The eyes and smile of the child masked the pain she must have endured. Jake looked at the photo of a younger Patsy Greenburg and realized he had treated her.

"Patsy, I couldn't care for you, but you can bet I'm going to take good care of your daughter," he whispered, lightly touching the faded photo.

Aside from pictures, Patsy had saved a few items of clothing that must have belonged to Macy through the years. There was also a blanket, a small knit cap Jake knew newborn babies wore in the hospital, and even Macy's ID bracelet from the hospital.

"Amazing," he sighed. Patsy had saved all these things from her time with Macy, but there were no other personal effects from her time after giving her up to the system. It was like, in Patsy's eyes, her life ended when they took her child.

Jake carefully put everything back in the box and replaced the lid. Carrying the box as if it were the crown jewels, he turned off the light and walked out of the office. He thanked the young girl at the front desk and left, putting the box in the trunk of his car.

As he drove back to Hope Springs, Jake knew he had to do something with all this other than just hand Macy a box of stuff. He couldn't just tell her what he'd found out and expect her to forgive him. But more importantly, he needed to show her that she was better than "good enough".

About halfway home, Jake knew what he wanted to do. And he knew just the group to help him pull it off.

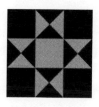

Chapter 37

"Okay, ladies, we've once again been tasked with a secret mission," Rosie told the members of the Advice Quilting Bee at their emergency meeting on Monday night. "Chandler isn't with us because it's her job to keep Macy out of here, so she doesn't find out."

"Also, this particular quilt requires complete confidentiality," Myrtle stated. "You can't tell ANYONE!" she ordered, emphasizing the last word.

"Okay, we get it," Fran huffed. "Get on with it so we can get busy."

Rosie began emptying the contents of the box. "This is going to be a memory quilt for Macy. Without going into all the details, I'll just tell you that her mother passed away recently and left this box of Macy's things. Jake picked it up when he was in the city and brought it to us. Mary Ann scanned the photos into the computer and printed them on fabric to incorporate them into the quilt. We also thought we could make blocks with the clothes and the blanket."

Once everything was on the table, Rosie pointed to the newborn cap and bracelet. "Does anyone have an idea of how we can incorporate these as well?"

The ladies all looked at each other, and Hillary shouted, "I do!" She ran toward the front of the store, where Rosie stocked a small supply of silks and bridal fabrics for her clients who liked to make fancy doll dresses. Coming back with a bolt of sheer netting, or bridal illusion, Hillary used it to cover the items. "I saw this in a magazine, where a woman made some sort of pocket for items that couldn't be sewn on. She sewed the illusion onto a background fabric. Then, after encasing the item on all four sides so it wouldn't fall out, she trimmed it with a coordinating grosgrain ribbon."

"Perfect!" Myrtle shouted. "Okay, everyone, let's divvy up the work."

Fran looked at the pile. "I'm almost afraid to ask, but when does Jake want this?"

"Well," Rosie hesitated, "considering Macy is barely speaking to him and won't until she knows the whole story..."

"ASAP," Fran answered.

"I think he wants to be able to present her with the general idea by Thursday night," Mary Ann told the group. "Let's see if we can get all the squares done and placed on the portable design wall by then. That way, she'll get to see everything even if it's not finished."

"That's a good idea," Rosie agreed. "I don't think Jake will be able to wait much longer, especially since they work together all day. I'll let Jake know the plan."

While the ladies were working at Rosie's shop, Chandler's job was to keep Macy occupied. Since they hadn't seen each other since the wedding, Chandler decided an evening at Macy's would be a good idea. She'd heard some talk from bakery customers about Macy and Jake not speaking to each other. She grabbed a bottle of Merlot from her stash, kissed Peter goodbye, and headed across the street.

"Okay, tell me what's been going on," Chandler ordered when Macy opened her door. "I brought wine," she stated the obvious, holding up the bottle for Macy to see.

Macy looked around Chandler to see if there were any of Myrtle's spies, or Jake, lurking in the shadows. "Okay, but inside tonight. I don't need Myrtle's spies hearing all my business." Macy stepped aside for Chandler to enter.

"Good Lord, we were only gone a week!" Chandler cried, "What could have possibly happened to cause you and Jake to break up?!" Rosie hadn't gone into detail when she'd asked for her help in keeping Macy occupied. Chandler just knew the basics.

Macy led her into the kitchen so they could pour the wine. Still on the kitchen table, where they had been since Friday, were the letter from the halfway house and the pink envelope. Macy handed Chandler the corkscrew while she got two glasses from the shelf.

Once they both had a full glass and were seated at the kitchen table, Macy showed the letter to Chandler. As Chandler read it, Macy could see the sadness and compassion on her face. "Oh, Macy, I'm so sorry about your mother. But I don't understand. What happened with Jake?"

"Didn't you read the letter?" Macy cried. "Jake knew about my mother and never told me!"

"I see," Chandler commented. "And that was reason enough to break up with him? Did he explain why he never said anything?"

Macy couldn't believe Chandler was taking Jake's side. "He said he never spoke to anyone about me and knew nothing about it."

"But you didn't believe him." There had to be more.

"No, I didn't," Macy said defiantly. She could tell Chandler had more on her mind. "Okay, let me have it."

Chandler took a sip of her wine, trying to figure out how to word what she wanted to say. "Macy, this one lie isn't the only reason, is it?"

Macy was quiet for a long time. Chandler knew her better than anyone in the world. She was more like her sister than just a friend. Macy took a sip of her wine and explained that, yes, there was more. "Rosie thinks I'm just using this as the excuse because, in my mind, I know that I'm not good enough for someone like Jake."

"What are you talking about!?" Chandler wanted to shake the girl. "Didn't you say that you told Jake all about your parents and the foster homes and the rest of it?" Seeing Macy slowly shake her head yes, Chandler continued, "And didn't you say that he told you he loved you anyway?!"

"Yes, he did," Macy cautiously confirmed.

"And you still doubt your worthiness?" Chandler asked, confused.

Macy put her face in her hands. She just wanted to scream. "Oh, why did my parents do this to me?!" she anguished. "How could they do this to a little girl?"

Chandler took Macy's hands away from her face and forced her to look at her. "Honey, believe it or not, your parents did you a favor." Seeing the look of shock on

Macy's face, she continued. "Your life was a living hell with them, but they gave you a gift. They gave you the strength and determination to want to make sure your life didn't turn out like theirs. If you'd all stayed together, you probably wouldn't be where you are today."

Macy removed her hands from Chandler's and took a long drink of her wine. What Chandler said did make some kind of sense. She may have ended up just like her parents instead of in Hope Springs. Maybe she wasn't so bad after all.

Chandler picked up the pink envelope. "You haven't opened it?" she asked. "Is this from your mother?"

"Yes," Macy confirmed. "Apparently, she mailed it to my old address before I moved, and it was returned to the halfway house where she was living. They sent it with the letter."

"So, she sent this over two years ago?" Chandler questioned. "Are you going to open it?"

Macy got a small smile on her face. "I'm almost afraid to. The last time I saw her was around that time, and as I told you, it didn't go well. I don't want to read again about what a brat I was."

Chandler laid the envelope back on the table. "You'll know when the time is right."

"That's what Rosie said," Macy smiled. "Okay, enough about me. I need some happy news. Tell me about your honeymoon!"

They spent the next hour in the living room finishing off the bottle of wine while Chandler told her all about how wonderful Miami was. And to Macy's surprise, she was

246

enjoying hearing all about how happy Chandler and Peter were.

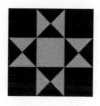

Chapter 38

On Wednesday, Macy was beginning to think something was going on in town that she wasn't supposed to know about. As she walked to the bakery to get some breakfast before work, she spotted Myrtle and Fran hurrying into Rosie's. It was eight o'clock in the morning! And they were looking around like they didn't want to be seen.

That afternoon, she saw Hillary and Andrea coming down the sidewalk as she left the medical center. She thought they were coming to see her, but instead, they quickly ducked into Rosie's. When Macy went to the shop, Mary Ann was locking the front door. "Oh, we have to close early," she shouted through the locked door. "Plumbing issue."

And by Thursday, even the ladies in the medical center were acting weird. Suzie just kept smiling at her all day, and Mary refused to speak unless it was about a patient. Jake was the only one who wasn't acting differently. Their relationship had gone back to the way it had been when they'd first met. They only spoke when it was about a patient.

Thursday evening, all Macy wanted to do was take a hot bath and climb into bed. Working with Jake all week and acting like everything was okay was exhausting. She knew the Advice Quilting Bee was meeting, but she decided to go home.

When Macy got home, the pink envelope was still on her kitchen table, unopened. For some reason, she was immediately drawn to it. She thought she heard a voice behind her say, "Macy, it's time to open the pink envelope." When she turned around, there was no one there. She sat down and opened the envelope.

"Oh, my," Macy whispered out loud. It was a card from her mom congratulating her on her graduation. But it was more than that. "Dear Macy," she read out loud, "For some reason, when I saw you, I couldn't tell you in person what I'm telling you now. I am so proud of you for the beautiful young woman you have become despite your father and me. You have done so much better at raising yourself than we could have done."

Macy stopped to wipe tears from her eyes so she could see to continue. "I've been fortunate to meet someone here who has shown me there is good in this world. He's too young for me, but he'd be perfect for you. I pray every night that you would find someone just like him. He's a doctor here in town, so maybe your paths will cross one day." Macy turned the card over as her mother had finished on the back. When she read the name of the doctor, she screamed out loud.

She grabbed her purse, keys, and the card and raced across the street to Chandler's. Banging on the door, she prayed Chandler answered and not Peter. "Oh good, you're home!" Macy shouted, looking past her. "Are you alone?"

"Yes, Peter's meeting Joshua and Keith for dinner. My goodness, what's going on?" Chandler asked, pulling Macy in and shutting the door.

Macy shoved the card in her face, "Read this!"

After Chandler read the card, front to back, she looked at Macy. "She sent him to you?!"

"It appears so," Macy smiled. "Now, how do I get him back?!"

Chandler grinned. "Let's go ask the group. I'm sure you'll get all kinds of suggestions."

When they entered Rosie's for the Advice Quilting Bee, Macy fully intended to tell the group everything and ask their advice. But they had other plans.

"Chandler, how was the honeymoon?!" Myrtle exclaimed. "And don't leave anything out!"

"Oh, yes," Rosie agreed. "I've been meaning to come by the bakery and ask, but we've been so busy."

"I know, I have too," Fran concurred.

Chandler began telling them all about how wonderful Miami was, how warm the water was, and the fantastic food they ate. Everyone kept asking questions, and before Macy knew it, the time had flown by, and it was almost nine o'clock.

Macy was just about to bring up the topic of Jake, which she was shocked no one had asked about before when Myrtle stated they were done for the night. "No!" Macy all but shouted. "I need advice from you guys about my relationship with Jake! You all know we broke up, and I'm frankly quite surprised no one had brought it up!"

Rosie, sensing Macy was getting quite upset by the whole thing, motioned for Mary Ann to wheel out the portable design wall. "Macy, dear, you may want to take a look at this," she told her, taking Macy's hand and leading her to the wall. "It's not completely finished yet, but we thought you'd want to tell us where you'd like each square placed."

Macy was speechless. The wall was covered with twelve blocks depicting her early years. As she looked at each block, she saw pictures of her younger self, fabric from a blanket she remembered and wondered what had happened to, and clothes she'd remembered wearing. But when she got to the block with her newborn cap and hospital bracelet, the tears started. She carefully traced the outline of the cap with her finger.

"Where?" she asked Rosie. She couldn't get any more out than that one word.

"I think there is someone here who can answer that better than I can," Rosie told her, turning her toward the front of the store.

Jake. Macy put her hand to her mouth to stifle a cry. She took a deep breath before continuing, "Where did you get this?"

Jake came to stand beside her and took both her hands in his. "I went to the halfway house to get an explanation about the letter. They had talked to Suzie, but only to get your address. They didn't divulge the reason for the call, just that they had something for you. Marge, the social worker, gave me a box containing all of these items. Your mother had saved it all. Marge wanted me to make sure to tell you that your mother loved you more than anything and wanted to make sure you received everything she had saved from your childhood." He angled his head toward the quilt. "As I was going through everything, I saw a photo of your mom. It was then that I remembered treating her a few times when I was a resident there."

251

Macy let out a little cry, and so did Chandler. "What's wrong?" Jake asked.

"She really did send him to you," Chandler whispered to Macy.

"What do you mean?" Myrtle asked, clearly confused, as was everyone but Chandler and Macy.

Macy went to her purse and pulled out the card from her mom. She held it up for everyone to see. "The pink envelope," Jake and Rosie said at the same time.

"What about the pink envelope?!" Myrtle demanded.

Macy smiled a big, tear-filled smile. "This is from my mom. She sent it over two years ago, but to my old address after I'd moved, so I never got it. It came with the letter from the halfway house informing me of her passing. In it, she told me how proud she was of me for all that I'd overcome and for the beautiful woman I'd become."

"Hallelujah!" Rosie exclaimed. "Do you finally believe you're good enough now!?"

Macy shook her head up and down. "But that's not all. She also told me that she'd met a young doctor who'd come to treat her at the halfway house. And he'd shown her there was good in the world. She'd said he was too young for her but would be perfect for me. She hoped our paths would cross one day. And his name was Dr. Jake Grainger."

That did it! Everyone was crying, and tissues were being handed out by the handfuls.

"Wow!" Jake whispered, trying not to cry in front of a room full of women. He certainly didn't expect that!

"Jake, I'm so sorry I ever doubted you," Macy apologized, wiping tears as she went. "I hope someday you'll be able to forgive me."

"Well, seeing as how your mom sent me to you, I think that can be arranged," Jake smiled, taking her by the hands again. "I certainly don't want to go against her wishes." He reached into his pocket and then got down on one knee.

There was an audible gasp in the room. Macy smiled and waved her hand at everyone, silencing them.

"Macy Greenburg, you are an amazing, strong, and very independent person, and I wouldn't have it any other way." He opened the tiny box in his hand, displaying the most beautiful ring Macy had ever seen. "Will you please do me the honor of becoming my wife?"

Macy looked around at all her friends, wiping their eyes, just like they had done for Chandler's proposal. Looking back at the man she loved more than anything, she said, "Yes, I will." After putting the ring on her finger, Jake stood up and kissed his bride-to-be while everyone dried their tears and cheered.

Later, as everyone was leaving and standing out on the sidewalk, Macy asked Rosie and Jake a very important question. "Would you both please go with me to the cemetery on Saturday to see my parents' graves?"

"Absolutely." Rosie hugged her.

"Definitely," Jake agreed. "We have to make sure we have their blessing."

Macy looked up at the Heavens and saw two shooting stars. "I think we already do." She smiled, hugging Jake close.

Epilogue

As they stood beside Macy's parents' final resting place, Rosie placed a small bouquet between the graves. "You both did do something right," Rosie spoke. "You brought Macy into our lives."

"Thank you, both," Jake added, kneeling. "I will spend every day for the rest of my life loving your daughter the way she should have always been loved."

"Thank you, Momma, for sending Jake to me," Macy whispered through tears. "Even after everything, I still love you both, and I hope you know that." Macy let out a little cry when they saw two white butterflies fly off from behind the small headstones.

"They know that, dear," Rosie told her, squeezing Macy's hand.

Later, after they'd dropped Rosie off at her house, Jake and Macy went back to his place. As they stood on the front porch, Jake asked Macy, "Are you sure you want to come in my house? It's haunted, you know," he teased.

Macy gave him a worried look. "I don't know. Maybe we should go to my place."

"No way!" Jake laughed, opening the door for her to enter.

They looked toward the kitchen and saw Maggie and Horace by the back door, plain as day. The older couple gave them a wave and then vanished through the back door.

"Huh," Jake said, staring at the empty space.

Macy wasn't sure what she'd seen but decided to play along. "Guess you're going to have to clean your own house now," she joked, reaching up to kiss him on the cheek.

Author Notes

I enjoyed creating the lively cast of characters who live in Hope Springs, Virginia! I hope you enjoyed them as well. Please consider leaving a review at Amazon.com. Since I'm an independent author, I rely heavily on my readers to spread the word. Any feedback you can give will be helpful to future readers.

Also, be sure to follow me at www.jenniferskinnell.com for future release dates on the next installment of the Advice Quilting Bee/Hope Springs Romance Series. Thanks so much!

Love and Happy Reading,

Jennifer

Made in the USA
Middletown, DE
06 April 2023

28374522R00154